When

Your

Heart

Mends

Books by Marilyn Peveto

PINE CURTAIN CHRONICLES

When Your Heart Comes Home
When Your Heart Mends

PINE
CURTAIN
CHRONICLES

When

Your

Heart

Mends

To Martha,
My long time friend—
Love, Marilyn

MARILYN PEVETO

Dedication

Dedicated with much love to
my husband, Alan; my children, Alison and Kyle;
my son-in-law, Doug; and my granddaughter, Lily Anna.

Chapter One

Pineville, Texas, March 1907

Sarah Andersson tipped her head back and turned her face to the heavens. There was just something about a cool morning, complete with sunshine and a cloudless blue sky. And if she wasn't responsible for guiding the wagon and horses down the road, she would keep her face skyward on this beautiful day.

It wasn't like they had experienced a long, hard, winter. Not in the piney woods of East Texas anyway. They may have tired of the gray winter dampness, but Sarah couldn't say it had been difficult.

No, she couldn't put her finger on why she awoke with such a bounce in her step, but she had a hunch it had to do with the definition of newness. A new season, full of hope for renewal in nature and in her own life.

Sarah clucked to the horses, who didn't require much urging this morning. They too, had extra energy, and it wasn't because they sensed it in her. When Mr. Thompson, the stable hand, brought the wagon around to her front gate, the horses stepped higher, so she spotted their vitality right away.

Besides, the weather was near perfect, so the dirt roads didn't cause the wagon to jolt and jog as she moved along. Of course, the rain had come in just the right amounts after January passed, affording an opportunity for the deep ruts to dry and smooth over.

The journey to town seemed like a quick mile, and before she knew it, she had crossed the railroad tracks. There were folks on both sides of the street, coming and going out of the mercantile, bank, and café at the hotel.

Pineville had been laid out in an orderly fashion, unlike some of the neighboring sawmill towns. The storefronts were all built from yellow pine lumber from the mill and were flanked by wide, wooden boardwalks to allow ease of movement by the townspeople. Each shop had an ample front window so the merchants could display their wares or advertisements.

Business was unusually brisk for a weekday. Of course, the majority of the shoppers this morning were the good ladies of the community because the Adams sawmill, the primary employer for the town, was well into its workday.

Mr. Wright, owner of the mercantile, was on the wooden sidewalk in front of his store, sweeping away the dust and the dirt that always found its way there from the street. When Sarah passed, he raised his hand to wave.

Sarah moved on through town toward the sawmill. She didn't have to be at the mill this morning, but she tried to visit the business she owned at least a couple of times a week. Since her mill manager was such a competent one, she was able to spend much of her time with her two small children and that was what she wanted most of all. When she drew closer to her destination, the manager at the mill, Thomas Carson, came to her mind.

Not only was he the one responsible for things at the sawmill, Thomas happened to be the man she planned to spend the rest of her life with. Her skin tingled just a little. Hopefully he wasn't too busy to visit when she arrived. Of course, he would make time for her if he possibly could. He always did.

When her destination was in full view, the noise of lumber production greeted her. Huge logs crashed into the mill pond from the railroad car while the band saws screamed in unison. Thomas was out on the log deck, standing where the timber traveled up the chute and onto the conveyor. He turned back into the building, and that signaled he was on his way to his office.

She climbed down from the wagon and smoothed her light blue skirt, then straightened the collar of her white shirtwaist. This was her first day to dress without the dark clothes of mourning. Seven months had been long enough to wear the drab, dark colors. Besides, in her opinion, garments alone could never attest to the amount of grief a widow experienced.

She walked to the offices that were located at the side of the structure. Thomas promptly stepped out and held the door for her. "Perfect timing, wouldn't you say?"

Sarah smiled and studied his face for a second. She wanted to reach up and plant a kiss on his cheek, but she didn't dare. Not at the mill.

They moved down the hall to Thomas's office. The warm finish on the pine floors almost glowed when met with the light from the large window. He motioned for her to sit in the chair nearest his desk. "I'm sure glad to see you this morning. And you look beautiful. Radiant."

"Thank you." He probably didn't realize she had shed the darker clothing of mourning, he just knew there was a difference. After all, he would never have asked her to do so.

Sarah placed her handbag on the desk. "I say I have to visit down here to see how the business is going, but I think I have other reasons too."

Thomas smiled and winked at her. "Since you mentioned it, I'd like to say things are going just about as well as they can be here. I've been tracking our production for a while. We're at the maximum level of board feet of lumber we can produce every day. Later on we may decide to expand, since the demand is steady and the timber is plentiful. Of course, we don't have to decide about that today."

Sarah leaned back in the chair. "And we've been blessed with good weather and a woods crew that can get those logs here to us.

My grandfather always reminded me of that essential element of mill production."

"I'm glad you listened to your grandfather. It helps that you know so much about the business."

Sarah turned to look at Albert Adams's photograph on the wall of the office. "You couldn't be with my grandfather and not learn something about this sawmill."

Thomas stood and Sarah knew it was her signal to let him get back out in the mill. She rose from her chair. "I know you need to get back to work and I have some things to take care of in town since Eliza is with the children. Will you be over for supper tonight?"

Thomas patted her arm. "Yes I will. I may go home first and get the smell of pine resin off me. But I'll be there." He lowered his voice. "It's my favorite place to be, you know."

Her heart fluttered just a little. "Well, I'll be going. And I look forward to this evening."

Their hands touched when they moved to the door. But the pact they had made, to honor her late husband's memory by not showing affection in public, kept her from stealing a kiss.

Supper waited on the stove while Sarah and the children watched for Thomas on the porch. When he came around the curve in the road, sitting atop his black horse, Blaze, she didn't say a word to Melissa and John, but she waited to see who would catch a glimpse of him first.

John ran to the picket fence as fast as his two-year-old legs would carry him when he saw Thomas. "Here he comes."

Melissa shrugged. "I saw him, too, John." Poor Melissa couldn't help but be preoccupied with their six-month-old puppy, Gus, since the cur tugged on her skirt every chance he got.

Once Thomas reached them, he grinned. "Looks like quite a group waiting to welcome me."

He secured Blaze and walked through the gate. When Sarah met him on the steps, he kissed her on the cheek.

"Supper's on the stove. I have to admit I didn't cook the chicken and dumplings or the buttermilk pie. I did make the cornbread, though."

"Well, you know I like all of the cooking you and Eliza do. And I especially love chicken and dumplings."

Motioning for them to follow her into the house, Sarah forged ahead. "Let's eat before it all gets cold."

She didn't get to say anything else to Thomas for the next few minutes, because the children walked along with him and chattered about anything that came to mind. Smiling, she strolled on to the kitchen.

Once she put the food on the table, Sarah removed her apron and clapped her hands in the air. "Everyone sit down, so Mr. Thomas can bless our food."

Sarah and Thomas joined hands before he prayed. Once he ended his prayer, the conversation among all of them began once more and continued until it was time to put the children to bed.

Before Sarah could take the children upstairs to put on their cotton nightgowns and clean some of the grime away that they collected in their normal daily activities, she led Thomas to the library to wait for them.

"Melissa and John love your stories. While I'm dressing them for bed, why don't you decide on a special tale?"

Thomas nodded and smiled. He had begun planning his story already.

Once the three of them had trudged up to the bedroom and made preparations for sleep, they appeared again in the library, and found Thomas ready and waiting. He had claimed the overstuffed arm chair and his hands were folded. The smug expression he wore suggested pure confidence.

John talked about horses more these days, so she wasn't surprised when Thomas decided to tell them a story about the first horses he and his brother, Paul, were given. Sarah almost giggled at Thomas's need to factor in more action than the story contained, but it turned out to be a good one.

Since Melissa and John sat still during the story, they easily drifted off to sleep. Thomas carried Melissa up the stairs while Sarah took John in her arms.

When the children were settled in their beds and Sarah knew they were fast asleep, she and Thomas tiptoed downstairs and into the parlor to visit. They situated themselves comfortably on the settee while the gas lamps in the sconces on the wall emitted a soft glow in the room.

Thomas reached over to move her long brown hair aside, and pull her closer. "If we didn't need to be near Melissa and John, this would be a wonderful night to enjoy sitting in the swing on the front porch. The weather has been gorgeous all day."

"Yes, it would. Do you think we could hear them from out there?"

"No, I don't want to risk it. There'll be other times to be outside since spring is nearly here."

Sarah rested her head on his shoulder. "Just think, someday we'll be together all the time."

Thomas sighed. "I'm ready for that day, Sarah."

They sat in silence, happy to be together, thankful for moments such as these. Because try as they might, these times were few and far between.

Chapter Two

S arah caught the porcelain cup just before it hit the floor. Who in the world would be pounding on her door so early? She steadied the cup and sat it back on the saucer. Before she could make her way to the front door, the thunderous knocks came once more.

She rushed toward the door to open it before the racket woke the children. She pulled the lace curtain back from the sidelight to catch a glimpse of her visitor. All she saw was the back of a man's head.

Sarah opened the door and he turned to face her. "Sheriff Walker. I didn't know who could be at my door."

"I'm sorry, Mrs. Andersson." He removed his Stetson and held it in front of him with both hands. "I really need to find Thomas Carson. Have you talked to him today?"

"No, I saw him last night but he hasn't come by this morning." Sarah stepped out onto the porch and closed the door. "Is there a problem at the sawmill, Sheriff?"

"No. No problem there." The sheriff sighed. "I checked to see if Thomas was at the mill before I came here. He was probably on his way. I'll check there again before I ride all the way out to his farm."

Sarah wiped coffee from her hand onto her skirt. "I'll tell him to contact you when I see him, Sheriff. That is, if you haven't seen him before then."

"I'd be much obliged if you'd do that, Mrs. Andersson. I surely need to talk with him."

The sheriff turned and walked toward his horse without another word, then he rode away in a cloud of dust. Sheriff Walker was acting very peculiar this morning. And why was he so desperately needing to see Thomas?

She let herself back in the house and headed upstairs to check on the children. When she peeked into their bedroom all she saw were closed eyes and the steady breathing of peaceful slumber. Back to the kitchen she went to resume her morning routine, relieved that Melissa and John had not been affected by the early morning visitor.

Settling into the chair at the kitchen table she wrote her list for the trip to Wright's Mercantile. When Eliza came to work this morning, she could finalize it, because her housekeeper always remembered something Sarah forgot to add.

She glanced down at her dress. She had spilled coffee in several places, so she would have to change before she left the house. But for now, she sat in her chair, buttered her warm biscuit, and reveled in the quiet of the morning.

If things weren't amiss at the sawmill, the visit from Sheriff Walker probably had to do with something that happened the night before, possibly involving some of the hands at the mill. Whatever it was, Thomas would take care of it.

She glanced out the window and caught sight of a yellow jasmine vine on the fence. If a wall didn't separate her from the flower, the heady fragrance would be so pleasant. My, how time moved forward. Could it be spring already?

Suddenly the sound of heavy footsteps on the back porch shattered the quiet morning. She rose from her chair and made her way to the door. Before she touched the knob, Thomas burst into the room.

"Thomas, good morning. Sheriff Walker came by earlier..."

Before she could finish the sentence, Thomas grabbed her in

an embrace. "I just talked with him."

He curled his hands into tight fists.

"Thomas, what is it?"

He motioned for her to sit at the table, while he pulled up a chair and sat beside her. He raked his hands through his hair before he spoke. "Sheriff Walker had a visit from a man last night that works at the state penitentiary up in Rusk. The warden from the prison sent him this way to deliver a message."

He took her by the hands before he continued. "The warden knows Sheriff Walker and used to live in these parts years ago. The sheriff says the warden also knew my family back then, so he figured I may be around here somewhere. Anyway, a convict by the name of James Watts was released a couple of days ago and is headed down to Beaumont."

"Watts? Is he any relation to the man you…?"

"Yes, he is. He's a brother to the man I…I killed in Beaumont." Thomas closed his eyes and shook his head. "Sheriff Walker says his visitor told him last night that Watts is headed to Beaumont to find me." He hesitated. "To avenge his brother's death."

"But you only killed him in self-defense. You would never have taken someone's life otherwise."

"I know. But he doesn't care about that. Sheriff Walker says this Watts fellow is a rough one. The sheriff doesn't want anyone to get hurt."

Sarah's lips trembled. "Oh, I'm so afraid for you."

Thomas released her and sat back in the chair. "That's just the problem. I'm not afraid of the man, but I am afraid for you and the children. And well, anyone else that gets in his way. He'll go to Beaumont first and see I'm no longer there. Then he'll find out I'm in Pineville."

Her eyes filled with tears. "Maybe he won't."

"Oh, he will." Thomas nodded. "I told everyone I worked with about Pineville and about my farm and how I couldn't wait to get back home."

She studied his face for a moment. "Well, the sheriff will just have to ask him to leave town if he comes here."

"I guess he can do that. But I'm not taking any chances. If he wants me he'll have to find me somewhere away from here." Thomas rose from the chair. "I'm leaving town in a couple of hours. I talked to Charles Griffin down at the depot and he's sending a telegram to your Uncle Marshall and Aunt Abigail in Jefferson. They'll be here soon to stay with you, and that way Marshall can assume my role at the mill until I get back. I'm headed now to make some arrangements down there."

Sarah's stomach churned. "Are you sure this is the best thing to do?"

He pushed his shoulders back and inhaled deeply. "Yes. I won't stay here and take a chance on having a showdown with this man and cause innocent people to be hurt."

Sarah recognized the look of dogged determination in this man she loved so deeply. She could never change his mind.

"Who do you think should be in charge at the mill until Uncle Marshall gets here?"

"I'm thinking George White would be the best one for the job. His son, John, is there to help, too. He and Marshall can work together because I know how your uncle hates to be in charge."

Sarah nodded. "Where are you going?"

"Into the Big Thicket. But don't tell anyone just yet. The only other ones I've confided in are the sheriff and Charles Griffin. Since Charles is the depot manager, I told him the facts of the situation so he could send the telegram to his mother and Marshall." Thomas let out a sigh. "I'm hoping Watts will come looking for me and get away from Pineville."

Sarah shivered. "I'm so afraid for you."

Thomas grabbed her shoulders. "Don't be, Sarah. I'll be fine. I have a friend where I'm going. And hopefully I won't have to be gone long."

Thomas's eyes glistened. "May I go upstairs and look in on Melissa and John? I won't wake them."

"You can wake them if you like."

"No, I don't want them to see me. They may sense there's a problem. The best thing for everyone is for me to get out of town."

Sarah stood even though her knees were weak. "Let's go upstairs together."

Thomas grabbed Sarah by the hand when they started up the stairs. She held back her tears when he stood beside the children's four poster beds and smiled. His tall frame bent ever so slightly above their soft feather mattresses while he peered at them. His dark eyes somehow matched the intensity of his black hair and Sarah loved the hue of both. But most of all, she loved how the light shined through his eyes, almost like a flickering candle, especially when he smiled.

He left the room and she followed. Once they were at the base of the stairs he stopped and wrapped her in an embrace. "You know I love Melissa and John like they're my own flesh and blood. And I know you'll take good care of them, but whatever you do, don't let them out of your sight."

Thomas pressed his lips to hers. "Goodbye, Sarah. Maybe I won't be gone for long. Until Watts makes a move, we don't know what he has in mind. Just remember, I love you."

She brushed his cheek. "I will. And you must think of how much I love you, too." There was an ache in the back of her throat. "How will I know how you're doing? Will you be able to send me word?"

"I'll try to let you know how things are. Just be watchful."

Thomas turned back again before he reached the door. "Oh, and if for some reason Watts does come here asking questions, tell him where I'll be. If he gets to Pineville, he'll need to be told where I am so he'll leave. Remember, don't do anything to put yourself and the children in jeopardy."

Thomas walked onto the porch, down the steps, and made his way to his horse. She forced herself not to run to him and stop him from leaving. He was right. He had to go. There were so many other things to consider besides their being apart. Yes, her mind said he had to go. But her heart ached for him.

Chapter Three

Sarah sat in the kitchen and watched out the back window for Eliza. She was a little numb from the events of the morning. And rightly so. How could she have ever imagined the news she would receive before her day even began? Hopefully, she could let Eliza in on the news about Thomas and his plans before the children awoke. Melissa and John would have to be told of his absence, but shouldn't hear the details and be fearful.

She would tell the children that something came up, and Mr. Thomas had to go away to visit a friend. That explanation should suffice, and it was the truth, even though it lacked critical elements regarding the situation. But they were elements a nearly three- and five-year-old should be spared.

She moved the list she had been working on. Once she filled Eliza in on what had happened, she would head over to the sawmill. It was important that she talk with George White and assure him she would be available to assist him at the mill when she was needed. Even though she owned the Adams Sawmill, she never intended to be there every hour of every workday. A mill manager like Thomas was invaluable to her since her children were always her first consideration, and he made that possible. And now that he was away, she would have to temporarily change her routine.

Even with the current upheaval, she was blessed. Two of her closest friends from childhood helped her accomplish the things she needed to do. Thomas was always there for her when they were growing up, then he arrived in Pineville just as her world crumbled with the death of her husband Nils, the father of her children. Then, soon after she became a widow, she was presented with the task of buying the sawmill her grandfather had built years ago, so the town could remain as it was. Thomas stepped up to the job as mill superintendent and all was well there.

Or had been until this morning. Thomas was not just important to her as the mill manager. They had a long history as friends, and hopefully, a future together.

Then there was Eliza, her housekeeper who had been with her as an employee for several years now. But before that, she was a friend. Eliza's mother had been the housekeeper for Sarah's grandmother when they were children. Some of her fondest memories were the times she and Eliza played together in the house and down by the creek that ran beside her home. Now she trusted leaving her children with Eliza when she had to spend time away.

Just then the back door opened and Eliza marched into the kitchen. "Good mornin'. I enjoyed coming over here today for sure. The redbud trees and dogwoods are startin' to bloom out in the woods and it's a sight I never get tired of. Every year it looks prettier than the last."

"Eliza, why don't you sit down for a few minutes before you get started. We need to talk."

Eliza's smile faded and she sauntered toward the table. "What is it? You look a might peaked this morning."

"I'm all right. Something has happened, though, that we need to discuss."

Eliza sat in the chair across from Sarah. "Oh, Eliza. Let me get you some coffee. I'm sorry. My mind is just racing."

Eliza touched Sarah's arm to stop her. "I'll get coffee later. I wanna hear what you have to say."

Sarah blinked back tears. "Thomas is leaving town this

morning. Sheriff Walker received news that the brother of the man Thomas killed in Beaumont may be looking for him. This man—James Watts—has just been released from prison and is expected to try to find Thomas to avenge his brother's death."

"Oh no. Lord help us." Eliza bowed her head,

"What I need you to do, is to be very careful here at the house. Do not open the door to any strangers. And we can't let the children outside unless we are with them."

Sarah closed her eyes for a few seconds. "I don't know what this Mr. Watts has in mind. We may never see him, but we must be prepared."

Eliza pressed her lips together. "You know I'll watch out for Melissa and John. Don't you worry."

Sarah pushed her chair back and stood up. "I need to go to the sawmill to check on things. I'd better go on and change clothes."

She paused beside the staircase in the entry hall. She clung to the bannister and uttered a prayer. "Our heavenly Father, please keep us safe. And please protect Thomas from this evil man."

Sarah took a deep breath before she walked into the mill's office. She wanted to present a facade of calmness to the employees, even though she felt like her insides quivered. Besides, it wouldn't be good for them to know the depth of her despair.

Without a doubt Thomas would have a clean desk top. He always paid attention to the incoming orders and any correspondence that arrived. And he spent an ample amount of time in the mill, helping with the production of lumber when he could. Thomas was the mill superintendent any company, large or small, would be proud to have.

Of course he had taken on this job for the same reason she had. They both wanted to keep Pineville the thriving hometown they had always enjoyed. If the owner after her grandfather had sold to a company that cared very little about the town, or if he had closed the mill, it could have changed Pineville completely.

Sarah sat at her desk and looked around the room. For the next few weeks at least, she may be needed here to oversee things in Thomas's absence. She was prepared to do that. She could only hope this ordeal would be over quickly and safely, so they could all settle back into the life they enjoyed.

Just then George White appeared at the door to her office. "Mr. White, please come in."

He removed his hat and came to stand in front of the desk. "Thomas talked to me this morning before he left town. I'm prepared to do whatever I need to do."

"I'm very grateful you are willing to help, Mr. White. I suppose Uncle Marshall will be back in town soon, but we all know he doesn't enjoy being in a supervisory position."

George chuckled. "We all know how Marshall is, but everyone here respects him, and likes him."

"Well, I'm going to count on you to oversee things in the mill while I try to take care of the office." Sarah shook her head. "And I only hope Thomas can be back with us soon."

"I understand. I'm going to get back to work, Mrs. Andersson. Our production here won't lag, I promise. If there are any problems and you aren't here, I'll send for you. But you know, things usually run pretty well around here."

"I appreciate that fact. Other mills in the area can't say that, you know. I'm truly grateful for the hard work here at Adams Sawmill."

After Mr. White left, she took a moment to decide who else she should discuss things with. Thomas had probably spoken with Clyde Morgan, the bookkeeper, before he left, but she wanted to be sure. She tapped on his office door and waited for his response. Mr. Morgan was known to get so absorbed in his work that he didn't like to be startled. Finally she heard him say, "Come in."

He rose from his chair and walked around the desk when she entered the room. "Mrs. Andersson, come in. I thought you were just someone interrupting my work again. Have a seat."

"Hello, Mr. Morgan. I didn't want to interrupt you, and I want you to know I truly appreciate your diligence."

"Thank you. I get so absorbed in my figures that I lose track of what's going on around me."

She settled in the chair in front of his desk. "I won't take much of your time this morning. I wanted to be sure Mr. Carson had spoken with you and explained his absence."

"Yes, he did. Frankly, I'm kind of worried about what this may mean for him. But I do know Thomas has a good head on his shoulders, and I think he'll come out all right."

"I have all the confidence in the world in his judgement. This is an unusual set of circumstances, however." Sarah pushed a stray strand of hair behind her ear. "I don't plan to be here every day, but I will be coming down more than usual. George White will oversee the operations in the mill, and I trust you can take care of the office when I'm not here. If you'll leave all the orders and invoices on my desk, I'll look over them."

"Yes, ma'am. I'll be glad to help any way I can."

"If you think there's something I should be aware of and I'm not in the office, please have Mr. White send for me."

She returned to her office and sat for a few minutes, staring into the distance. She was amazed at the difference one day could make. Only yesterday, she visited here with Thomas. Their conversation centered around the production at the mill and plans for supper. Now Thomas was gone, and the responsibility of the mill was all hers for the time being. She pushed her sleeves up closer to her elbows and concentrated on the orders and invoices that came in this morning.

She tried so hard to pay attention, but her thoughts kept

gravitating to Thomas. How she wished he didn't have to be alone right now. Each time her mind wandered, she pulled her thoughts back to the work at hand. Once she waded through the paperwork, she was up to speed with the affairs at hand.

When everything was in order, she walked out of the office. Thomas was facing so much. She had to trust that everything would be all right in the end, but her fears were great at this moment. A chill passed over her even though the bright sun shined on her shoulders.

Chapter Four

Thomas tipped his hat to the attendant at the ferry when he reached the other side of the Neches River. So far his plans were falling into place. He had camped on the Jasper county side the night before, then he rode over to Sheffield's ferry at the first light of day. Fifteen cents was a small price to pay to cross the river that remained a bit swollen after the recent rains.

When he left Pineville the day before, it had been a grueling stretch of travel before him to make it to the river by nightfall. That was a goal he had set for himself to be able to make it to the thicket by tonight. So, when he made it to the Neches and finally stopped for the evening, he ate the biscuits and bacon he had hurriedly packed before he left home. Sitting on a bluff above the water he had prayed, thanking God for his safe travels and making a humble request for the protection and well-being of Sarah and the children. Then, when the sun lowered itself behind the pines, he fell onto his bed roll in an exhausted state.

His weariness wasn't just fatigue from physical exertion that day, but a mental weariness, too. The shock of finding out James Watts was on his trail, the hasty goodbyes and instructions at the sawmill, made him more tired than if he had worked a twelve-hour day in the logging woods.

Now he wondered how the creeks would be on the way to his destination. He would come to Hickory Creek next, and hopefully it would be easy to maneuver. Blaze seemed eager to move ahead and Thomas decided his horse looked forward to a little adventure.

It would take several hours to ride into Hardin County where he would locate the trail he remembered close to Honey Island. Thomas squinted when he looked at the sun. He had to get into the Big Thicket before nightfall. It was hard enough to make his way through the thicket in the daylight, much less finding Solomon's house when darkness settled in.

Solomon would be surprised when Thomas got there since there was no way to send a message. His friend had little or no contact with the outside world. Solomon would have to leave the thicket to go to the nearest post office, so he didn't bother with that but every once in a while. He also didn't need to visit a mercantile in the towns near his home very often since he raised what he needed to eat or hunted for wild game. And of course, he fished in the river and the creeks.

Thomas hadn't seen his friend in two years, but theirs was a friendship that stood the test of time. Solomon would be glad to see him when he finally got there. He and Blaze moved on toward their destination.

When he neared Honey Island in the early afternoon, Thomas breathed a sigh of relief. A man could pace himself on these roads, but he had no idea how long it would take to travel once he made it to the Big Thicket. If the trail had grown up, it could be a time-consuming venture.

Now that he had arrived at the point of entry, the most important thing was to enter the thicket at the right place. A man could get lost in there forever. Thomas stood for a few minutes and looked at the small opening in front of him. Was it the trail or was it just a spot that had been beaten down? He studied it for a few minutes. There was the X that was carved on the oak tree. The palmetto bushes had grown so thick they nearly hid the mark he always looked for.

He urged Blaze onto the trail and tucked his arms closer to his side to keep from hitting the tree limbs all around him. Once inside the confines of the path, Thomas guided Blaze to a slow walk so they could move along with great care. It was as though he had left civilization as he knew it and was embarking on a journey to a land far away, even though he was still in East Texas, not that great a distance from his own home.

There was an eerie quietness, except for the snapping of branches as squirrels leaped from one limb to another. He smiled at the sweet song of a yellow-throated warbler, almost like it greeted his entrance to their abode.

Solomon's place was several miles into the thicket. It seemed farther because travel was slow, and because a man had to be keenly aware of his surroundings at all times. He touched his rifle that rested beside him. The very first time he and his father visited Solomon's family, a panther had jumped out on the trail and scared them half to death.

Thomas watched the dappled sunlight fighting to push its way through the leaves of the oaks, sweetgums and pine boughs. The shade was nice, but the absence of direct sunlight made it feel later than it was, and that had him pulling his watch from his pocket more often.

Moments later Blaze came to a complete stop, unable to go any farther. Thomas had been peering all around him at the thick forest, as the trail in front of them worked into a virtual wall. He turned and pulled the hatchet from the saddlebag, then climbed down to stand in front of Blaze. He hacked away at the branches of the oaks and sweetgums, and then some of the underbrush, until he cleared a path to move through.

When they could make their way down the trail again, they moved along. There was no way to hurry the process, even though Thomas was ready to get settled in and rest a bit.

The news of James Watts wanting to find him hit hard, for sure. He had finally put some of that part of his life behind him. Only some of that part of his life, of course. Even though he had finally allowed himself to accept God's forgiveness, he could never forget the act of killing another man.

Thomas pulled on the reins to stop Blaze while he inspected a small baygall that appeared in front of him. The standing water didn't look too deep, but the dank smell of the slough filled his nostrils. He decided to check it before crossing. Once he was on the ground, he found a limb from a pin oak to put in the hole and measure the depth. Since it was passable in several places from his measurements, he urged Blaze into the swampy ground and they moved forward without much effort.

Pushing through the wet area, Thomas spotted a mayhaw patch blooming with its dainty white flowers. Visions of gathering the berries each year with his family when he was a boy ran through his mind. Just the thought of his mama's mayhaw jelly made his mouth water a little.

They were soon back on solid ground. His knees hit trees on both sides as the forest became more dense. The woods swallowed the trail. The daylight waned, so he became hopeful when he saw smoke rising from a cabin up ahead. As he drew closer, he saw the smoke wasn't coming from the mud chimney of the house but from a fire out front. At the sight of his friend skinning a buck, a smile crossed Thomas's face. He stopped Blaze right there.

"Solomon Brown. Is that you?"

Solomon never looked his way. "Would you be the likes of Thomas Carson?"

"Yes, I would."

A black mouth cur ran toward Thomas, barking as to warn his master of danger. Solomon moved to a pan of water to wash up. "Enoch, let him pass. He's a friend."

The cur dog obviously understood the command, because his tail began to wag. Thomas climbed down from the saddle and faced Solomon, who stood with an outstretched hand.

"What brings you out to the thicket?"

"I was hoping I could visit with you for a spell." Thomas glanced down at his muddy boots. "The truth is, Solomon, I've run into some trouble. And I need a place to hide for a few days so I can plan the best way out."

"Well, you've come to the right place. You know I'm ready to help." Solomon wiped the sweat from his brow with his sleeve. "It's a little hot up by that fire." He patted Thomas on the back. "Let's put your horse out in the fence with mine. Have you eaten anything since you got on the trail?"

"No, I was waiting to find you. I didn't want to stop and let the night catch up with me."

"Good thinkin'."

Solomon motioned for Thomas to follow him with Blaze. They walked in silence out to the barn.

"I'm going to put him out here. There's water in the trough and I'll throw him a little feed."

Solomon took charge of Blaze and gently patted the horse in the process.

"Let's get back up to the house. I suspect you'll want to go on in and eat something while I finish with this buck I killed a little while ago. We can talk when I get back in."

Thomas followed the orders his friend offered. Solomon was that kind of man. He assessed a situation and knew right away what was needed.

"You'll find sweet potatoes, cornbread and some venison backstrap on the stove. Eat all you need, and I'll be in later."

Thomas let himself into the house and placed his hat on the rack by the door. He washed his hands with the lye soap and rinsed them with the water he poured from the pitcher by the sink. He opened the cabinet and found the plates in the same place as last time. Nothing had changed much since he was here before.

It was two years ago that he had been here to hunt with his friend. And they had roamed the woods for days. That visit was

29

before the incident with James Watt's brother. Now he would have to recount the painful details of the ordeal in Beaumont when he killed a man to keep from being killed. But Solomon would understand.

If anyone could help him sort through the grave situation he faced now, it would be Solomon.

He sat down and took a bite of the backstrap that was breaded with a mixture of coarse cornmeal and a little flour, and pan-fried. It was good to be in the home of his friend where he could finally relax. But right away his thoughts turned to Sarah.

How long would he have to wait for Watts to come for him? He prayed it wouldn't be long. He already missed Sarah, and he hadn't even been gone but a couple of days. He had to watch his step now that he was involved in this trouble. He couldn't let his judgement become impaired due to his missing Sarah. And that would be hard for him, because he loved her more than he had ever loved anyone.

Chapter Five

After Sarah and the children tucked their packages in the wagon, they strolled down the wooden sidewalk in front of Wright's Mercantile. She had promised them lunch at the hotel once they completed their errands in town. Besides, Eliza could finish her work at the house so much easier without all of them underfoot.

"Mama, look. There's Uncle Marshall and Aunt Abigail." Melissa ran toward them. Sarah loosened her grip on John's hand, knowing he would want to do the same.

Uncle Marshall stopped in his tracks when he saw Melissa and John headed their way. Abigail stopped and grinned at the children, but they were headed for their great-uncle first.

Sarah finally caught up with the children. "Uncle Marshall, what are y'all doing back in town so soon?"

Abigail moved past Marshall and the children and caught Sarah in an embrace. "We came on the first train headed this way. When we received the message from Thomas, Marshall and I grabbed our suitcases and packed."

"I'm so happy to see you but I didn't expect you to get here so quickly. And you both look wonderful. Married life is obviously agreeing with y'all."

"Thank you. You look wonderful, too." Abigail pointed down the street. "Marshall was headed over to the livery to get a wagon but now we can put our things in yours."

"And the children and I were going to the hotel for lunch. This is perfect. We can all go together."

Uncle Marshall put his hand on John's shoulder. "We're hungry for sure. We can get something to eat and then head home to get settled in."

Abigail situated herself between Melissa and John while they walked toward the hotel. Uncle Marshall and Sarah walked a few steps behind them. "I feel awfully bad that you and Abigail had to come home. But we've surely missed both of you."

"Wouldn't have it any other way, Sari. We couldn't get here quick enough. You don't know how glad I was to see the three of you walking toward us just now."

Abigail and the children entered the hotel lobby while Sarah and Uncle Marshall stayed on the porch. "As soon as lunch is over, we'll get our things from the depot and head home. Once I help Abigail settle into our room, I want to see Sheriff Walker. I need to find out if there's been any word from this James Watts."

"I haven't heard anymore from the sheriff." Sarah tapped her uncle's arm. "I have to admit I'm happy to see you and Abigail, even though I'm sorry you had to cut your trip short because of these circumstances."

Uncle Marshall rubbed the back of his neck. "We'll plan what we need to do about the situation later this afternoon. Right now let's all enjoy a good meal."

Sarah and the children sat on the second seat of the wagon while Uncle Marshall and Abigail shared the first. Uncle Marshall was her grandmother's youngest brother and had always been with them. Since he was only ten years older than her own mother and had no children, he regarded her like his own daughter.

She studied the back of her uncle's head and his shoulders. He never aged. He had always worked at her grandfather's mill, and the hard work kept him fit. Besides that, his brown hair was still thick and wavy, and according to Abigail, he didn't look much different than he had at sixteen.

After losing her parents when she was only two years old, her grandparents made sure she was loved and cared for. Once her grandparents were gone, Uncle Marshall had stayed on with Sarah and her late husband, Nils. Now her children loved Uncle Marshall like the grandparent they never had.

Sarah felt John's head against her arm. He had given in to the slow rocking motion of the wagon and fallen fast asleep. She glanced down at Melissa, but she stared ahead and probably was planning all the fun she would share with her Uncle Marshall and Aunt Abigail.

Both of her children favored their late father so much. Their blonde hair and blue eyes were exactly like his. That first day she had met Nils in Wright's Mercantile, his quick smile emphasized his clear blue eyes and his blond hair, lighter than any blond she had ever seen, framed his oval face. She had been smitten.

They rounded the curve on the road leading to her home, and the twin brick chimneys rose into the air. Not only were the brick chimneys majestic as they towered over the landscape, but they were responsible for pulling the smoke from eight fireplaces in the house during the winter months.

She had lived in the beautiful home her grandparents built here in Pineville from the time she was two years old, and now it belonged to her. Her mother had been Albert and Averill Adams's only child so Sarah was the lone heir to their holdings of money and land. With the gifts she had been given, much responsibility was involved. And that was why she now owned the sawmill.

When the owner of the mill decided to sell, he offered it to Sarah first, because her grandmother had included that clause in the contract when she sold the sawmill after Sarah's grandfather died. Her grandmother had been wise to insist that the mill be offered to Sarah, their only living descendant, if he ever decided to sell.

Word had gotten around that a buyer from up north was interested, and there was a certain reputation that absentee owners possessed. Oftentimes, mill owners who weren't interested in the town built around the enterprise would come in, cut the timber out, then close the mill. Albert Adams had built the mill and the town around it before Sarah was ever born. Her job now was to see that the town thrived the way it was intended.

When her home came into view, a thrill ran through her. The white paint on the gingerbread trim that adorned the wrap-around porch and second story balcony was always so clean and fresh against the light gray color. Of course, her grandmother had chosen the colors for the paint and trim when the house was built many years ago. Sarah never considered changing the colors on the exterior of the house because they were perfect, nestled in among the trees.

Her grandfather planned the setting carefully, with large oaks surrounding the house, providing much needed shade, and tall pines towering behind, creating the perfect backdrop.

When they finally arrived, Uncle Marshall pulled the horses and wagon to the gate and stopped to let them enter. "I'll take these harnesses off and brush the team up, then I'll be in directly."

"Oh, I haven't told you, but I hired someone to work outside after you and Abigail married. Mr. Thompson can take care of the horses."

"Is that Mr. Earl Thompson?"

"Yes. I thought you probably knew him. He gave up the mill work a few years ago due to his age but he's still able to do the things I need here."

"He's a good man. Last I heard he was doing odd jobs around these parts. This is a good arrangement for him and you."

"And so far, it's worked well. I know you'll want to talk to him a little, but let him take care of the horses. We'll see you in the house in a bit."

Abigail stepped down first, and Sarah handed a still-sleeping John to her. Sarah and Melissa then joined Abigail on the porch. "Sarah, I'm glad you reminded Marshall that Mr. Thompson can care for the horses. He'll have a hard time letting go of the things he used to do here."

"I know. I was so happy when you and Uncle Marshall married. But I figured out pretty fast that I'd need someone to help outside. Uncle Marshall did so much for us."

Sarah held the door for Abigail. "I'll let Eliza know we're here, then I'll take John upstairs to his bed."

Sarah moved part of the way down the hall to the kitchen before she called out to Eliza. "We're home. And guess who's here?"

Eliza emerged from the kitchen with an iron skillet still in her hand. "I just looked out the window and saw your Uncle Marshall out back. When did he get here?"

"Just a little while ago. He and Abigail arrived on the train around noon."

"I know you're happy to see them. I'll feel a lot better if they're here at night."

"You're already worrying about us. Please don't."

"You have no idea what kind of man that Mr. Watts is. You said he's been in the state prison up in Rusk." Eliza turned to head back to the kitchen. "I'm not just worryin'. I'm prayin', too."

Once Sarah placed John in his bed to finish his nap, she joined the ladies and Melissa in the kitchen.

Abigail patted Melissa's shoulder. "This sweet girl is going to help me unpack our things in Marshall's room and get our clothes in the chiffarobe."

"Oh, don't you think you and Marshall will be more comfortable in one of the larger bedrooms upstairs?"

35

"No, we already discussed it. You know he's an early riser and loves to get the stove fired up and coffee made." Abigail chuckled. "Trust me, Sarah. You'll be glad you let us stay downstairs."

The back door closed and Uncle Marshall walked into the kitchen. "Looks like 'ol Earl is doing a good job."

Uncle Marshall grinned at Eliza. "Hello. Sure is good to see you. How's Frank?'

"He's doin' good, Mr. Hensley."

"Melissa is going to help me get our things put away, Marshall. Did you bring our bags in?"

"Earl is bringing them to the porch. He insisted."

"Uncle Marshall, you have to let him work. Soon you and Abigail will be headed back up to Jefferson, and I'll need him for sure then."

Uncle Marshall glanced over at Abigail. "We finished everything we needed to do in Jefferson at Abigail's home place. We were headed back this way soon, anyway." Uncle Marshall rubbed his hand across his face. "We were both tired of being away from you and the children and from Charles. Isn't that right, Abigail?"

"That's right. I had already written Charles and let him know we would be back soon. He was a bit surprised when we stepped off the train today. I believe we arrived sooner than he thought we would. Surely sooner than the letter I wrote. And I think he's missed his mother a little, but he won't admit it."

Abigail moved next to Melissa. "Are you ready to help Aunt Abigail? And Marshall, I think Sarah is ready to talk with you."

"Sari, let's go sit on the front porch. How about it?"

Sarah followed her uncle out the door. "I'm going to talk to Sheriff Walker in a little while. Charles told me the sheriff visited him over at the depot and asked him to be on the lookout for this Watts." They sat in the rocking chairs. "Says he's a rough character."

"I wonder why he was in the penitentiary."

"The sheriff told Charles he was charged with attempted murder."

A chill ran down her spine. She closed her eyes for a second. "So, Thomas was probably right to leave town. I'm still worried about how this will end, though."

"I know you are. But I have all the confidence in the world in Thomas and his judgement on matters like this. And of course, he'll have time to think where he's going." Uncle Marshall shook his head. "We'll take care of things here and Thomas will take care of what comes his way. Try not to worry."

"It's hard not to. But, I do want to make sure the children aren't fearful. There's no reason for them to have to know everything. It was only seven months ago that their own father left to return to Sweden and died before he ever got out of the United States."

"You're right. We won't discuss any of this around them."

She would accept his advice. They would take care of things here. She had to concentrate on that fact. Right then and there, she stopped and prayed that Thomas would be safe with his friend, and that her heart could be a little lighter. Because right now, it weighed a ton.

Chapter Six

Sarah felt almost naughty when she waved goodbye to Eliza and the children and guided the wagon down the road. Uncle Marshall had asked her not to go out alone during this uncertain time. She had convinced him no one wanted to accompany her to the sawmill every day, so he conceded that the usual trip to the mill was the exception. Sarah had not objected. She had nodded and smiled, but it would never work.

She was not abiding by the wishes of her family by striking out alone, but she needed some time at the Pineville cemetery. It wasn't something she did often, but this morning she craved the peace she received from visiting the final resting places of her mother and her grandparents.

She wouldn't be gone long, and besides, this James Watts wasn't even in town yet. And there again, he may never even make his way to Pineville. So, this morning she had slipped away after telling Eliza she needed to check on something at the mill. And she did plan to stop by there after she spent a little time at the cemetery.

She followed the road past the school and the church and waved to Brother Maxwell when she saw him leaving the parsonage. She couldn't resist stopping to talk for a minute, so she guided Lucky and her small wagon to meet him. He was always busy in the Lord's work and she was so thankful her grandfather had brought him and his wife, Beulah, to Pineville years ago.

"Good morning." As she moved closer, she called out her greeting.

"Why, good morning, Sarah. You must be headed down to the cemetery. Either that or out of town."

"I'm headed to the cemetery. I needed a little time alone this morning, and sometimes I like to visit down there and you know, just think, and maybe talk a little to those who've gone on before me."

"I understand completely. This time of year, I notice there are always more visitors down there. I don't intentionally keep a record, but I see folks going that way." Brother Maxwell rubbed his chin. "I think it's because the weather is nice, and spring brings forth such feelings of renewal and hope."

"I guess I have a habit of going this time of year, because my grandmother always did. As soon as the blooms started to form on the trees and plants in early spring, she'd start planning bouquets to take to the cemetery." Sarah chuckled. "I am so much like Averill Adams. I can't deny that."

"Yes you are. And that's a compliment." Brother Maxwell looked toward the road. "You know, I see people coming and going as I make my way back and forth from my house to the church building. Most folks wave as they go by, or some stop and say hello, and I've lived here long enough to say I know most everyone, whether they attend church here or not. But the other day, a man stopped when he saw me outside and asked if he had taken the right road to get to the cemetery. I assured him he had, but I'd never seen him before. I introduced myself, but he never did tell me his name. He was nice, but didn't want to divulge much information. In fact, he never would say who he had buried here."

"That is odd. Oh well, he was probably related to someone who used to live here long ago. Hopefully he found the cemetery all right." Sarah waved. "I'd better get on down there myself. Good day, Brother Maxwell."

Before long she arrived at the cemetery that sat in a clearing, surrounded by a cluster of tall pines. Once she lifted the lock on the gate, she eyed the stone that bore her mother's name, *Katherine Elizabeth Smith*. What would life have been like with her father and mother had they not died from influenza?

Her grandmother told Sarah her mother became ill, so Sarah's father sent her to Pineville to protect her from becoming sick. Her father, Andrew Smith, was a young physician who had begun a practice in Coldspring. Sarah's mother had died from the malady first and Sarah's grandfather traveled over to San Jacinto County and brought his daughter's body home. He had not gotten to visit with his son-in-law, Andrew, because he was gravely ill, running a high fever, and not wanting to pass the influenza to anyone else.

It always bothered her grandparents because they only received a letter several weeks later from a friend of her father's saying he had passed away and was buried there in Coldspring with other victims of the influenza outbreak. Sarah's grandfather had tried to contact the friend for more information but never received any news. He then sent an employee of his to try and gather the details of his son-in-law's death and burial, but no information could be found.

She was at peace with the circumstances because her grandfather had tried to get the facts concerning her father's death. And besides, she had lived a wonderful life in Pineville.

Sarah stood a moment beside her mother's grave then between her grandparent's. The dogwoods, yellow jasmine and honeysuckle were beginning to bloom so Sarah would be bringing bouquets soon to lay on each grave, just as she had done in years past.

A light breeze blew around her but not enough to move the pine boughs. She smiled at the beautiful sunshine beaming down. Nature was preparing for a beautiful show—spring in East Texas.

She turned to leave, then blinked twice. Did she see something move in between the trees across the road? Or was it someone?

Chapter Seven

Thomas woke to the unmistakable thud and sloshing cadence of the churn. He sat up in bed and called to Solomon, "Good morning. I must have slept too long."

"Good mornin'. There's no such thing as sleeping too long. When a body's not on a tight schedule, we get the rest that's needed."

Thomas joined Solomon in the kitchen. "Mind if I get a cup of this coffee? It sure smells good."

"The cups are on the shelf to the left. I ground the coffee beans this morning so it's fresh and flavorful. And by the way, I generally get up early because I like to get my chores done so I have time to fish or do things I enjoy. I needed to get this butter churned while it's still cool outside. Now that we're into March, there's some warm days."

Thomas poured a cup and added a little sweet cream from the shallow dish left out after the morning milking. "You never tire of life out here, do you?"

Solomon's lips parted in a grin that moved his beard from being the focal point of his face for a moment. "There's everything I need here. And plenty of it. I go into town about twice a year but I don't need to go any more than that. Besides, I have neighbors a few miles through the woods."

Thomas grinned. "How will you ever find a Mrs. Solomon Brown way out here?"

"And I haven't heard of a Mrs. Carson yet."

41

Thomas set his coffee cup down and sighed. "I hope to marry sometime this year."

Solomon rose from the chair. "Let me wipe the cream from my hand so I can shake yours. Congratulations, Tom."

"Thank you. I'm happy about it all. But I've got to move past this obstacle first." Thomas motioned for his friend to sit beside him. "If you're ready, I'll fill you in on the story, but it'll take a while."

Solomon returned to his chair. "I'm ready. Let me hear it."

Lightning flashed around Thomas and Solomon while the thunder crashed. Thomas ducked his head and stayed behind Solomon. The trees swayed in the wind. While they ran for cover, he had two fears. One was that a huge tree would fall on them and the other was that lightning could strike them while they ran.

Finally, they approached Solomon's house. They reached the porch and Solomon put down the string of fish he'd been carrying so he could shake the water from his clothes. Thomas did likewise. Every stitch of clothing stuck to their skin, drenched from the heavy rain. Thomas reached for the door while Solomon grabbed their catch of the day.

Once inside, Solomon smoothed the moisture from his long hair and grabbed a towel from the oak washstand to wipe his face. "Looks like we caught a good amount of catfish before the rain started in. At least now we'll be warm and dry while we cook it up and eat it."

"Those thunderstorms came out of nowhere." Thomas pulled a clean, dry pair of pants from his bag. "Yep, at least we have supper for tonight. Doesn't sound like the rain is letting up anytime soon."

Solomon dragged two iron skillets from the oak cabinet. "If

you want to cut up some taters, I'll get the fish ready."

"Sure, I'll be glad to help. We'll have ourselves quite a meal."

"You know, I've been thinking about your situation. If Watts makes it this far, you'll have to stand your ground. Seems like he'd learn a lesson, doesn't it?"

"Yes, it does. I've finally forgiven myself for taking his brother's life because I know the Lord forgives me, but the consequences of that sin just keep hanging around." Thomas looked off into the distance. "I don't want to face the thought of having to take a man's life again to save mine."

Solomon stroked his beard. "You need to pray that it won't come to that. My mama always said we wait to pray until after we exhaust all other avenues. I guess me and my dad did that a lot."

"I sure loved your mama and daddy. If our families hadn't known each other for generations, we wouldn't be friends today, would we? Unless I happened to meet you on one of your twice-a-year trips to town."

"Yes, I'm thankful our families have enjoyed such a long friendship. And we have to remember that we come from peace-loving folks. You never know about things, Tom. Maybe we can do some good with this feller. I hope we can. Because if we can't, I won't let him take you out. Trust me."

Chapter Eight

Sarah stood beside Abigail as she straightened her hat in the mirror in the entryway. Sarah, Abigail, and the children waited for Uncle Marshall to bring the wagon around to the front of the house. Abigail smoothed her collar, then turned to face them. "I'm looking forward to hearing Brother Maxwell preach this morning. I've missed his sermons while we were gone."

Sarah reached down to tuck John's shirt in one more time. "He does bring a good sermon, Abigail. He's loved in Pineville for sure."

Uncle Marshall pulled the front door open. "Let's go. We don't want to be late."

Sarah and the children settled into their place behind Uncle Marshall and Abigail, and they started down the road toward the church. There would be an empty spot on the pew where Thomas usually sat. Before she ever left her bedroom, she prayed for his safety this morning and she would continue that prayer until she knew he was free from harm.

When they reached their destination, Sarah's friend, Lucy Bailey, waited for her on the front steps to the church building. "I've missed you this week, Sarah. Since I've been helping my daddy at the office, we haven't had much of a chance to talk."

"I've missed you, too." Sarah leaned over to hug her. "Your blue eyes shine more than usual today with that shirtwaist you're wearing."

"Thank you. Mama found this for me when she took the train

up to Lufkin."

"I'd love it if you'd come over this afternoon and we can visit on the porch."

"I'll do that. I want to show you a swatch of fabric I recently bought and get your opinion on the trim. And of course, Daddy told me about Thomas." Lucy shook her head. "I hope that's resolved soon."

"Yes, we do have lots to discuss. I'll see you this afternoon."

Sarah always loved spending time with Lucy. After attending college in Huntsville, Lucy had accepted the job to teach at the school in Pineville starting in September. But for now, she sometimes filled in at her father's office in town. Dr. Benjamin Bailey had been the physician in Pineville ever since Sarah was a small child, so she and Lucy had been friends for as long as she could remember.

At least Uncle Marshall and Abigail were back in town with them and with her this morning for the church service. Also joining them on their pew was Charles Griffin, Abigail's son. Uncle Marshall and Abigail were thankful every day that Charles moved to Pineville to run the depot because it gave the two of them a chance to reconnect after they had known each other many years ago.

Sarah's mind went back to that day in church last year when Uncle Marshall took his place on the pew beside her, then his eyes lit up when he looked across the building and saw Abigail sitting there by her son. Her uncle sat during the service in a trance-like state. He would look over Abigail's way, then back again.

Sarah had caught herself gazing at the beautiful lady, too. Her blonde hair with a little silver above her ears and at her temples framed her lovely peaches-and-cream complexion. But her physical beauty paled in comparison to her inner beauty.

They all soon discovered that Uncle Marshall and Abigail had known each other many years ago when both their families lived up in Jefferson. Uncle Marshall's family had moved away, then when he came back to see Abigail a couple of years later, she had already made plans to marry Charles's father. Marshall had not made his intentions known when he discovered she planned to marry someone else.

Abigail married and moved to West Texas but lost her husband when he was killed by cattle rustlers on their ranch many years later. She and Charles had moved back to Jefferson to be near her family. When Charles was grown, he landed a job as the depot manager in Pineville. Abigail made a trip to help Charles get settled, and she was surprised to see Marshall Hensley after so many years. She and Marshall entered into a whirlwind courtship and married a few months later.

They sat as a family this morning, singing hymns, praying and listening as Brother Maxwell delivered God's word to them in a sermon. The only thing that could make this day better was if Thomas was here with them. How was he? She prayed he was safe and could be back with them very soon.

When the last "Amen" was said and they moved toward the wagon to go home, Alma Martin barreled toward Sarah. The townspeople must be discussing Thomas's plight, because no one asked where he was this morning. That was an indicator of the gossip in the tiny town. If someone had not known, they would have inquired about Thomas. When no one asked about him, she felt sure it was a good sign of how fast the news had traveled. And Sarah knew his absence from the sawmill had been explained on the job site. What in the world could Alma want to know?

She was nearly out of breath by the time she reached Sarah. Alma grabbed her by the arm as if Sarah were running away.

"I didn't see Thomas Carson in church this morning. I wondered if he could be sick, or has he left town?" Alma stopped talking only because she needed to catch her breath.

"He's away for a while. And no, I'm not sure when he'll be

back."

Alma steadied her gaze on Sarah. "I really wondered if he left town because he's running from that man or if there was another reason."

Heat rose in her face, but she held her composure. "I can assure you that he's not running, Mrs. Martin. He's trying to protect…Oh, never mind."

Sarah stepped aside and turned toward the wagon where her family waited. Fortunately, the children had walked along with Uncle Marshall and Abigail.

Uncle Marshall grinned as Sarah boarded the wagon. "A good dose of the town gossip?"

"I'm afraid so. I always think I'll be ready for her intrusive questions, but I never am."

"Abigail cooked up a delicious meal before we left this morning, so let's go taste it. What do you say?"

"Oh Marshall, I'm sure they get tired of you bragging about my cooking." Abigail playfully patted his arm.

"It's the truth. Nothing but the truth. I smelled that pork frying when I was upstairs getting dressed this morning." Sarah sniffed and closed her eyes to recapture the pleasant aroma.

On their way home to the scrumptious feast that awaited them, they passed through town, and as usual on a Sunday afternoon, the sidewalks were deserted. When they came to the hotel though, a stranger was tying his buckskin horse to the hitching post. The wagon slowed as Uncle Marshall took a hard look at the man standing there. The stranger turned and stared at them. The man's gaze fixated on Sarah and her heart fluttered. He needed to shave, and his face had settled into a hard frown. Sarah wanted to look away, but she couldn't. A scar stood out on the man's right cheek. Could this be James Watts?

Chapter Nine

A bigail walked in the front door and immediately removed her hat, placing it on the table in the foyer. "Marshall, the children and I are going to the kitchen. They love to help me set the table. Come along, Melissa and John."

Sarah nodded. She motioned to Uncle Marshall to join her in the parlor. "Do you think that man outside the hotel was James Watts?"

"I don't know. It could have been somebody passing through." Uncle Marshall wiped his hand across his forehead. "I tried to get a good look at him, but it all happened so fast."

"He was about your height, five feet eight or nine inches tall. Much shorter than Thomas. I guess he was medium build and he had a scar on his right cheek. He stared at us, but I couldn't see the color of his eyes."

Uncle Marshall stood from where he was seated. "Do we have a description of this fellow?"

"No, sir. Not that I know of anyway. But the scar, the unshaven face, the scowl. These things made him look like he fit the bill."

"I'll go on after lunch to talk to the sheriff. It may not be Watts at all, but I need to tell him about the man just in case it is. Well, let's see if we can help Abigail get that food on the table. I'm mighty hungry. What about you?'

"Yes, I am, too." But she had actually lost her appetite when she saw the stranger in front of the hotel. It had to be Watts. And he came for answers she wasn't prepared to give.

She went through the motions of helping to get their Sunday dinner on the table. Finally, they all took their seats, and Uncle Marshall blessed the food. She picked at everything on her plate, but no one prodded her to eat. She always loved Abigail's cooking, but today she just couldn't put the food in her mouth, chew, and swallow.

As soon as the meal was over, Uncle Marshall announced his intentions to visit Sheriff Walker concerning the man they saw in front of the hotel. "Charles, will you stay here with the women and children while I'm gone?"

"I certainly will."

Sarah started to protest but stopped. Perhaps it wasn't such a bad idea.

Abigail cleared the table and worked on putting the food away. "Sarah, you go on up and read to the children before their nap. Charles can help me clear this away, and I'll make some coffee. We didn't plan to have dessert until Lucy gets here anyway."

"Oh, I forgot about Lucy coming over. Thank you, Abigail, for reminding me. Yes, I'll take Melissa and John upstairs for their nap."

Sarah trudged up the stairs with a heavy heart. Only time would tell if this was the man they feared was looking for Thomas.

The children had been promised dewberry cobbler when they awakened, so they magically gave into the heaviness of their eyelids. Sarah didn't stay upstairs for long after she was certain they were asleep. She was making her way back down to the kitchen when she heard Lucy talking to Abigail and Charles in the parlor.

Abigail motioned for Sarah to join them in the parlor when Sarah appeared in the doorway. "Sarah, Lucy just got here, and Charles said you all should visit in here. He said Marshall told him not to allow us to visit on the porch today."

"He was pretty serious about the instructions he gave me, so I think we'd better abide by his wishes." Charles peered at each of the ladies when he spoke.

"I understand. He's always so protective of us. Lucy and I can visit anywhere, can't we?'

"Sure. But, I get the settee. This is my favorite piece of furniture."

Abigail and Charles retreated to the kitchen so she could make coffee and get the dessert ready to serve.

"Sarah, what has happened? Abigail and Charles were being mysterious but seemed to be a little fearful."

Sarah sighed. "I know you've been told the reason Thomas left town."

Lucy nodded.

"Today after church, we saw a stranger in front of the hotel, and Uncle Marshall and I are afraid it could be James Watts."

"Why? Do you know what he looks like?"

"No, we're probably being silly, but he stared at us really hard, you know. Of course, we were probably looking him over too, trying to figure out who he is."

"I'm sorry you have to be worried. Hopefully this can all be over soon."

"The sad thing is, it either gets over soon, or we'll have days like this every time a stranger comes to town. The sheriff had told Charles to watch out for him over at the depot. He thought he may come by train, but this man was tying his horse in front of the hotel."

Just then a rapping sounded at the front door. Gus barked and growled. Sarah rose from her chair.

Charles met her in the entry. He shooed her back to the parlor. "I'll get it."

She eased back but stood in the parlor doorway to listen.

"Who's there?" Charles asked.

"I'm looking for a Sarah Andersson."

"What's your name, sir?"

"Watts. James Watts."

Sarah's heart raced. Beads of sweat formed above her lip. It was him. How did he know to come looking for her? She moved forward. Was it the man she saw in town today?

Charles cleared his throat.

"Mrs. Andersson is not accepting visitors this afternoon."

He pounded on the door until it shook. Charles looked in her direction. "Marshall told me you know where his gun is. Get Marshall's gun. Hurry."

She scurried to the desk in the parlor. She drew out a revolver. Hers, the one her grandfather had given her and taught her to use.

Sarah caught sight of Lucy who sat frozen, her blue eyes wide.

"Go to the back stairway and up to the children's room. Stay there. And take Abigail with you."

Sarah moved into the entryway with Lucy behind her. Melissa came down the stairs, rubbing her eyes. Sarah gasped.

"Lucy, get Melissa."

Lucy jumped to retrieve Melissa from the stairs. Suddenly, the door gave way.

James Watts stood in the entryway.

Charles grabbed for the handgun. "Sarah, go with Lucy."

Melissa cried. Lucy grabbed Melissa and headed upstairs. Sarah's heart pounded. She stepped in front of Charles.

"Mr. Watts, whatever makes you think you can push your way into my home? Get back on the porch."

She motioned to him with the revolver. He obeyed her commands.

Charles grabbed Sarah by the arm. "Let me handle this."

"No. Charles. I won't have my children frightened this way."

She never took her eyes off Watts. "What did you want to discuss? And you'd better make it fast."

James Watts eyed the gun. "Where can I find Thomas Carson,

the coward that killed my brother?"

Sarah tightened her grip on the gun. "He is not a coward. He's with a friend in the Big Thicket."

A grin spread across his face, and his nose and upper lip worked into a snarl. "That's a pretty broad description. That thicket covers a mighty big piece of land. Did he go in at Honey Island, Batson, or some other place?"

"I don't know. But he's not here." Sarah fingered the trigger on the pistol. "You'd better not ever set foot on my property again. Do you understand?"

His mouth twisted like he had bitten into a persimmon that wasn't ripe. "Thanks for the news. I'm much obliged."

Chapter Ten

Sarah kept the pistol aimed at Watts while he walked outside the gate where his horse was tied. Gus barked and growled while following the man. Raising his foot to kick at Gus, he stared at Sarah.

"Don't do it, Watts." She waved the revolver in his direction.

As he rode away, a wave of nausea swept over her, while visions of Thomas ran through her mind.

Charles stood behind her. "I didn't want you to have to do that."

"Do what, Charles? Threaten a no-good man with a gun or tell him where Thomas is staying?"

"Neither." Charles looked down at the floor.

"Thomas told me to tell him where he is if it came to this. And I'm the only one who knows how I feel when a man like this comes to my home, threatening us that way. I won't stand for it."

After she placed the gun back in the locked drawer, she wiped her damp hands on her skirt. "The plan is working. James Watts will not rest until he finds Thomas. Now he'll leave Pineville and that's what Thomas wanted."

Abigail ran to Sarah's side. "Oh, Sarah, I'm sorry this happened. But I'm so proud of you."

"Thank you. I'm relieved that our part in this is probably over." Sarah's eyes filled with tears. "Where is Melissa?"

"Lucy took her upstairs and I suppose they're still there."

Uncle Marshall and Sheriff Walker burst through the front

door. "Sari, we believe that was James Watts we saw today. We talked to Lila Hill over at the hotel, and she said he was real friendly. Said he told her he was looking for an old friend, Thomas Carson." Uncle Marshall frowned. "She said he sat around there in the lobby after he had lunch, and he said he hadn't seen Thomas in a long time and wanted to visit with him. She didn't know any better and told him to come see you."

Charles pinched the bridge of his nose and sighed. "He's already been here. In fact, he just left."

Sheriff Walker patted his gun in his holster. "Which way was he headed, did you notice?"

Sarah smoothed her hair. "West, sheriff. Toward the Big Thicket. I don't think we'll see him around here anymore."

The sheriff rushed out the door.

Uncle Marshall removed his hat and banged his thigh. "I never should have left." He squeezed his eyes shut. "I can't believe I wasn't here for y'all."

"We managed everything all right."

"Looks like you did, Sari. But that's not what I wanted. I should've sent for the sheriff to come here after we saw Watts at the hotel. No, I was wrong to leave y'all here like that."

Sarah steadied herself on the handrail then headed up the stairs to find Lucy and the children. Her hands were still a little shaky, but then she took a deep breath. Mr. Watts wouldn't be back around. He would spend his time looking for Thomas now. Thomas would be ready, just as she had been.

Perhaps she and Thomas worked as a team even when they were apart.

Thomas peered out the window, the beautiful sun peeking through the pines. Sleep had not come easy for him the night before, and it wouldn't, until he could return home to the ones he loved. Waiting to see what would happen with Watts left him pacing the floors.

Solomon returned from his chores outside and grabbed a pouch from the sideboard. "Ready? I've got us something to chew on. There'll be plenty of fresh water to drink along our way."

"Yes. This is a good idea. I need to be familiar with these woods."

"You can't learn it all in a day, but I can show you the closest creeks and then some swampy areas you want to avoid. You never know when it'll come in handy."

"How far is your closest neighbor?"

"I'd say a few miles. We'll probably make it over to old man Cain's place by noon. There's a lot to look at on the way and maybe a few surprises, too."

"Surprises?"

"It's nearly spring. There'll be some water moccasins in the little ponds and other snakes, like the copperheads, laying right beneath the pine needles that share the same color."

"So you're talking about snakes?"

"Not just snakes. We may get the opportunity to see a panther or if we're lucky, a bear. They're all out there. And then again, we may not see any of those. Or we may them all. You never know what you may find out in the thicket."

"I'm ready, then. And I think that's what makes this place so special. Never knowing what to expect."

"For some it is. Some folks ain't too keen on the surprises, though." Solomon eased out the door. "We'll follow Cypress Creek a ways. It pretty much leads us to Mr. Cain's."

Thomas traipsed behind Solomon, drinking in the beauty of the forest. The dappled sunlight begged to intrude through the tree tops but was only allowed to shine in slivers.

Thomas let out a yelp when a magnolia branch clutched his arm between its leaves. Solomon stopped in his tracks. "What's up, Tom?"

Thomas rubbed his arm. "Nothing, I guess. I thought something grabbed me, but I think it was a tree branch." He examined his arm more closely. "Yep, tore a hole right there in my shirt."

"You're a might jumpy. You ready to move on?"

"You're going to laugh about this for days, aren't you?"

Solomon stroked his beard, and gazed off into the distance. "Probably not days. Maybe just one day."

Thomas walked along the trail in silence. Why was he already jittery? Watts may not even know he was in the thicket yet. But maybe he did.

After about a mile, they came to the creek bank. Frequent spring rains had made it rise, but it was not yet over its rim. The yaupon bushes were so thick in places a man would have to crawl on his knees to work through them, so they meandered down the trail that ran beside the creek, even though it was slippery in places.

Solomon wiped his forehead with his shirt-sleeve. "We've covered about two miles now, so let's stop here and get a drink. This is the place I know I can lean over and drink from the spring."

"Beautiful place, Solomon. But I guess you know them all."

Solomon chuckled. "When I think I do, I always run into another one. I stumble on new things pretty often."

After quenching their thirst, they resumed their walk. What would it be like to live in a place that held surprises every day? He'd settle for less of the kind of surprises he had now in his life for sure.

They finally came to a place where a split rail fence ran out in a grassy area. Solomon stopped and turned to Thomas.

"I want you to stay here while I go and tell Mr. Cain I've brought a visitor. He doesn't like strangers around his place."

"That's fine. You think he'll let me come up there?"

"Yep. I think so. His wife, Thelma, is one of the best cooks around. I'm hoping she has the noon meal just about ready."

Solomon returned after a few minutes. "He said to come on, he's ready to meet you. But I have to warn you, he's got a tooth that's bothering him, so he's trying to pull it out with the pliers."

Thomas walked beside Solomon, and finally, an inviting log house with a dog trot down the middle came into view. Sitting on the edge of the porch was a man holding a pair of pliers up to his mouth. His first glimpse of Clark Cain.

Solomon walked past the man and settled in a ladder-back pine chair on the porch and motioned for Thomas to take the matching one beside him. They sat quietly while Mr. Cain tugged at his tooth with the pliers.

When she emerged from the house, Thelma Cain wiped her hands on her apron. "When did you get here, Solomon? I'll bet you smelled the squirrel frying on the stove, didn't you? And I've got sweet potatoes and corn bread."

"No, I didn't smell it, but I already told my friend here that you'd have something cooked."

Thelma looked over Thomas's way. "I'm Thelma Cain. And you are...?"

Thomas rose from his chair. He should have risen when she first appeared on the porch. He had been keeping one eye on Mr. Cain. "I'm Thomas Carson. So glad to meet you, Mrs. Cain."

Suddenly Mr. Cain howled, then expelled a tooth in his hand. He leaned over the edge of the porch and spit a few times. "Finally got it. Won't be givin' me trouble now."

"Lunch is ready, Clark."

"Good, I'm hungry as can be."

Thomas filed in behind the others. How could Mr. Cain be so eager to eat after he jerked the tooth out of his mouth?

Thelma glanced over at Solomon. "Would you bless the food?"

Solomon nodded, closed his eyes and prayed.

Thelma passed the sweet potatoes around. "We love it when

Solomon comes to visit. He was always friends with our son Dan, so we got used to seeing him over here."

Mrs. Cain's voice was soft and sweet, and her eyes sparkled when she smiled. Thomas pictured her in a small town like Pineville, comparing recipes with the other ladies and discussing the newest fashions in clothing. How did she exist out here, living day in and day out with a man who hardly talked and was suspicious of anyone who came near his place?

Mr. Cain finally addressed Thomas. "So, you hiding from somethin' or somebody?"

Thomas felt the heat rise from his neck up to his forehead. Was it so obvious? "Yes sir. I guess I am."

Clark Cain sighed. "It's been happening for years. Way back in 1836, General Sam Houston planned to retreat to the Big Thicket with his troops if he'd not won at San Jacinto. There's truly nothing new under the sun."

Solomon came to Thomas's rescue. "I failed to tell you that Thomas is someone I've known for years. His father, Burl Carson, used to come hunt with my father. Thomas is here because he's pushed in a corner. I want to explain that someone might stumble on your place, looking for mine. Or someone might come asking questions."

Clark laid his fork down for the first time during the meal. "I don't take too kindly to strangers coming around asking questions." He looked directly at Solomon. "If you say this man is your friend, I'll help him out."

"Thank you, sir. I appreciate your concern." Thomas extended his hand to Mr. Cain, but the older man ignored it.

"The only reason I'm concerned is because Solomon says I need to be."

Solomon pushed his chair back and stood. "You won't be disappointed in this man, Mr. Cain. I can assure you of that." Solomon moved over to stand beside Thomas. "We'd better be on our way. Thank you for the wonderful meal, Mrs. Cain. We appreciate your hospitality."

Mrs. Cain came to their side of the table and hugged Solomon. She extended her hand to Thomas. "We hope to see you again, Thomas. Will you be in the Thicket for a while?"

"Thank you, m'am. I hope to see you all again, too." Thomas rubbed his arm. "I'm not sure how long I'll be here. If things work out well, I'll be getting on back home."

"Well, I'm sure you're glad to be able to spend a little time with Solomon. He's a wonderful man."

While laughing, Solomon retrieved their hats from the rack on the wall. "I'm not sure everyone sees me in the same light that you do, Mrs. Cain. But thanks, anyway."

Mr. Cain never moved away from the table. He watched them make their way to the front door. "We're here if you need us, boys."

Solomon waved. "See you soon."

When they got back on the trail, Thomas asked Solomon about the couple. "So, they seem mismatched, you know. She's so pretty and pleasant. He's just the opposite."

"Think so?"

"I sure do."

"Her family lived out here for years. Thelma's father didn't believe in the War Between the States. He wasn't a shirker, you know. He just had a problem with killing another human being over state's rights or slavery, so he hid out in the Thicket. Once the war ended, he and his wife decided to stay. They had created a life here that they loved. Thelma was born right there in the house where they live. People say she's just like her mama."

"That's interesting. I figured Mr. Cain forced her to come here." Thomas chuckled. "Guess I was wrong."

"I grew up with their son, Dan, so they're like second parents to me."

"Does Dan live here?"

"Nope. And he wants nothing to do with life out here. He always liked to read and study the books they had at the house, and his mama taught him all she could, but like me, he didn't have any formal schooling. Dan never liked to hunt or fish much like the rest of us. When he turned seventeen, he went to stay with his uncle in Houston and went to college. He owns some kind of business now. Has a wife and a couple of kids. Rarely ever comes home."

"That's kind of sad for the Cain's, isn't it?"

"Thelma took it better than Clark. She knows living out here isn't for everyone. Dan really resents the isolation he was brought up with. He loves the city and all it offers."

"I can see that he may prefer the city, but I'm sure his parents would love to see him and his family once in a while."

"Dan says that road runs both ways. Mr. Cain doesn't like to leave the thicket. Mrs. Cain doesn't like to leave her husband alone here, so she doesn't go visit without him. Maybe someday they'll get it all worked out."

Solomon stopped in his tracks. "Wait. What was that noise?"

They stood in silence, listening. Solomon moved toward a clump of undergrowth, thick and gnarly. "Hey little one. Are you stuck in there?"

Thomas inched closer. His friend pulled out a shivering little puppy. "Why are you all alone in there? Where's your mama?"

"Solomon. Look over here." Thomas turned his face away from the sight.

Solomon walked to the place where Thomas stood. "All right, little pup. Looks like your mama got caught by something pretty fierce. Probably a bobcat."

Solomon handed the puppy to Thomas. Thomas laid him against his chest. The puppy reached up and licked his neck. "Poor little thing. He's hungry, thirsty, and a little wet from hiding in those briars and bushes."

Solomon inspected the area around them. "Looks like he's the only one. His mama probably died protecting this little one. We'll take him home, clean him up and feed him." Solomon reached out for him. "I'll take him if you'd like."

"No. He's just fine here with me. I'll carry him."

Solomon pulled off his hat and scratched his head. "I know most of the people who live out here and the dogs they hunt with. I've not seen a hound like his mother. She probably got lost on a hunt and lived out here on her own. Wish I'd found her earlier."

Thomas pulled the puppy closer. After they got back on the trail the puppy stopped shivering and fell asleep. He felt his muscles relax and he walked a little slower. So, was this was the kind of surprise Solomon talked about earlier? It surely was a pleasant one.

Solomon stopped and leaned forward. "Panther tracks. We'd better watch out for the rest of the way home. They can spring at you when you least expect it."

The puppy may have stopped shivering, but Thomas couldn't.

Chapter Eleven

Sarah waited on the back porch for Mr. Thompson to bring the wagon around so she could go to the sawmill to check on things in the office. She would have left earlier since Abigail was there with the children, but she wanted to wait until Eliza came so she could explain what had happened on Sunday with Mr. Watts.

As she expected, Eliza was frightened by the account of all that took place. She advised Eliza they probably wouldn't have to worry about Mr. Watts anymore, but Eliza didn't seem convinced.

If only she could feel relieved that Mr. Watts was gone, but he was headed to find Thomas. She knew all too well Thomas had orchestrated this plan, but she couldn't help but feel uneasy.

Mr. Thompson pulled the horse and wagon to the porch so she could begin her trip to town. "Lucky is all ready, Mrs. Andersson. He's a pleasure to work with. I figured you just needed the small carriage since you're going alone."

"Thank you so much, Mr. Thompson. I want you to know I'm very pleased that you're working here around the place."

"Well, I'm enjoyin' it. Thanks so much."

When Mr. Thompson headed back to the barn, Sarah and Lucky started off at their usual pace. The morning train made its presence known when it came down the tracks that ran parallel to the road that Sarah travelled on to town. The engineer always began his warning signals there because it was one mile from the depot.

She was so accustomed to the noise of the train that she

sometimes didn't even notice it, but today, the rhythm of the wheels on the track and the hissing of the steam engine caught her attention. Ever since the altercation with James Watts on Sunday, her senses had been heightened. It was as though she had to be prepared for any conditions that were out of the ordinary. She didn't expect to see him again, but she had to be ready, just in case.

Still, her stomach sank. Thomas had told her to tell Watts where he was if he came around. And she had done just that. If she hadn't, Watts would probably still be hanging around Pineville, waiting for Thomas.

Why do I feel so bad? It's not like I had lots of options. Getting Watts out of town was something I needed to do. But then I sent him straight to Thomas.

There couldn't be a true winner in this situation after all.

The morning train had already stopped at the depot and the passengers were stepping down on the platform at the depot when she and Lucky finally made it to town. She parked the carriage as close as she could to Dr. Bailey's office and grabbed her handbag before she entered his office.

Maybe she would see Lucy this morning, even if it was only for a few minutes. She needed to see that her friend was not still shaken after the visit from James Watts. She expected to find her at the front desk. When she didn't, Sarah wandered down the hall. The doctor's usual assistant, Mrs. Travis, walked out of an exam room when Sarah made her way down the hall.

"Good morning. I thought I might find Lucy here today."

"Not today, Mrs. Andersson. Lucy and her mother had plans to do some shopping out of town. Doc Bailey is in his office, though."

"Thank you, I'll step in to see him."

She tapped lightly on the door and Dr. Bailey said, "Come in."

When Sarah entered the room, he rose from his chair. "Sarah, have a seat. I'm so glad to see you." Dr. Bailey peered over his glasses, studying her face.

"Lucy told me what happened yesterday. I know it had to be trying for you, regardless of the bravery you showed."

"It was trying and left me feeling not as secure as I have in the past. I realized Sunday afternoon that we have to rise to the occasion, however unpleasant it may be. Charles Griffin was a little upset with me because I didn't let him handle it, but I thought I was more incensed at the actions of this man than he was. He barged into my home and frightened my family." Sarah looked down at her hands. "And if something more had to be done, if he had not left on his own, I didn't want Charles burdened with the consequences."

"I'm amazed at your moral strength. Well, not amazed. I've watched you grow and continue to grow through each phase of your life."

"Thank you. You know how much it means to me for you to say those things. I'm sorry though, that this incident left Uncle Marshall feeling pretty low. He is angry with himself for leaving us there alone after seeing the man we suspected was James Watts in front of the hotel."

Dr. Bailey nodded. "Marshall and I both feel protective of you. He, because of the fact you are related and he actually looks at you as he would his own daughter. Me, for several reasons, one being you have grown up here right before my eyes and have been the best friend to my daughter. The second reason is that your father and I were close friends for a number of years while we were in college and medical school in Tennessee. To honor him, I feel I have an obligation as a friend to see to your well-being. Of course, I'm quite fond of you, too. You're like a part of our family."

"I feel blessed to have you and my Uncle Marshall to lean on now." Sarah glanced at the clock and rose from her chair. "I'd better be going. Since Thomas is away, I have to be in the office several times a week to give my consent on orders and other financial transactions."

"Things have surely gone well over at the mill since you purchased it. I'm thankful you were able to secure it and keep things on an even keel here in Pineville."

Sarah inched closer to the door. "I'm pleased that it's worked out so well. But I have great employees there. And I'm not sure how long it will be until Thomas returns but I'll feel better about things at the sawmill once he does. He makes running the mill seem effortless."

"I'm sure he won't be gone long. I have all the confidence in the world that he'll find the correct solution to this problem."

While Sarah made her way outside, Dr. Bailey's words stayed in her mind. Yes, Thomas would find the correct solution to the problem at hand. But oh, how she missed him and would love to hear from him.

She paused before she climbed into the carriage and looked up and down the streets in town. Sheriff Walker had told her not to worry because his office was on a constant look out for James Watts. And word had gotten out so that most everyone in town was keeping watch for a stranger. She stopped for a moment and said a prayer. Then she climbed up and took the leads and moved forward with new strength and peace.

Chapter Twelve

A faint whistling in the kitchen and the unmistakable thud of the iron skillet being placed on the stove awoke Sarah. Uncle Marshall. He must have already brought wood in for the stove and was cooking breakfast.

Yes, Abigail had been correct to insist they stay downstairs instead of in one of the larger bedrooms on the second floor. Sarah hurriedly brushed her hair and pulled on a calico dress so she could enjoy the morning with her uncle.

She tiptoed in the children's room and glanced at both of them. They slept soundly and peacefully, as children should. Hopefully, she could make their life full of joy and innocence just as hers had been.

By the time she reached the kitchen, Uncle Marshall had bacon frying in the skillet, and he hummed, but ever so softly, so as not to wake his beloved Abigail. So she didn't startle him, she cleared her throat. Her uncle turned as she pulled a chair away from the round oak table.

"I didn't think Abigail was up yet. Good mornin' Sari."

"I thought we could have some time to visit. I know this is your favorite time of the day."

"And I know it's not your favorite time. You couldn't sleep?"

"I guess I slept as much as I needed. If I only knew Thomas was doing all right, I suppose I could rest better. But I guess it's true that no news is good news."

"I've found that to be the case. If anything comes up that we need to know, his friend will find a way to contact us."

"I know you're right. I just wish things could be more settled."

"Well, when we get past this thing with Watts, and Thomas comes back home, I think we'll get back to normal."

Uncle Marshall removed bacon from the skillet and cracked eggs to fry. "How many eggs for you, Sari?"

"I guess just one."

"Me and Abigail have been planning to go out to my property on Saturday to lay out plans for our house. We want to get started soon, so we can be out of your way in a few months."

"Y'all could never be in our way. Melissa, John, and I love every minute the two of you are around."

"Well, we want to get moved in to our place before you and Tom marry."

"Marry? I guess we will eventually. We haven't made plans yet. Thomas knows I want to wait a respectable amount of time after Nils passed away."

"Yes, I know how you feel. One year is considered respectable and that will be here before you know it. I just want you and those young'uns to be happy. I've watched enough to know Tom Carson makes you all that way."

"Yes, he does." Sarah looked out the window and saw the sun peeking through the trees. "I can only hope he will be home soon."

When a knock came at the back door, Sarah and Uncle Marshall looked at each other. Uncle Marshall headed to see who it could be. "Good mornin', Earl."

"Mornin' Marshall. When I came up I saw something on the front porch. Whatever it is has a burlap sack around it. Thought you might want to see." Mr. Thompson wiped his hand across his forehead. "You know, since the sheriff said to watch out for anything suspicious."

"Yessiree. I'll go look. Thank you,"

"Do you know what it could be, Sari?"

"No. I don't remember seeing anything yesterday evening when I came home."

"Let me take up these eggs and I'll go look." Uncle Marshall put the eggs on the two plates on the counter and moved the skillet.

"I'll go Uncle Marshall."

"No. There's no telling what it could be."

"Well, I'm going with you." Sarah stepped in behind him when he walked from the kitchen.

The two of them moved out the front door. The burlap bag sat beside the rocking chair.

While he loosened the bag, Sarah stood back. Inside was a crock jar with a tag bearing Sarah's name.

Uncle Marshall stood back. Tears welled in her eyes. "That's Thomas's handwriting." She lifted the lid and looked inside the crock jar. "It's honey. Honey from the Big Thicket."

She grabbed the jar and started back in the house. "He always said the sweetest honey was in the thicket. And I believe he wanted me to know he's all right."

She pulled the crock jar to her chest. "I can't think of a better way to start the day."

Sarah didn't know how Thomas had gotten the jar of honey to her porch, but she remembered he said he would send a sign that he was doing all right. And he had.

She entered the house with a bounce in her step. Maybe this would all be over soon, and he would be back in Pineville. The jar of sweet, pure honey lifted her spirits and gave her more hope than Thomas would ever know. She sighed. After all the uncertainty and angst, it was a good feeling.

Chapter Thirteen

After they finished a fine supper of venison stew and cornbread, Thomas followed Solomon to the porch. The night sounds were surely different in the big woods. Wolves howled, owls screeched, and panthers screamed. Since the house was not even one hundred yards from the deep woods, the noise of the thicket had bothered Thomas at first. But he had grown accustomed to it, and he enjoyed the time they spent in the evening on the porch or around a fire in the yard.

Some evenings the gnats were so relentless, flying around their heads and entering their mouths when they tried to talk, that a smoldering fire with a good amount of smoke, was all that allowed them to stay outdoors. They built the fire near the fence where the horses were, so they could get relief from the gnats that tormented them, too.

This evening was one to be spent near the smoldering fire. Pulling two chairs closer to what was now mostly embers, they settled in to listen to what dusk would offer in the big woods.

"I guess Sarah has found her package by now." Thomas gazed into the distance, visions in his mind of Sarah finding the package on the porch and being delighted.

"If everything worked the way we planned, she should have the honey. I'm glad we met up with Mr. Jordan's boy and discovered he was headed out to make his deliveries. He sells to most of the stores in the larger towns. Everyone likes the honey from out here."

Thomas petted the puppy and watched for gnats that may try to buzz around her little head.

Solomon stretched his legs out and crossed his arms. "You're spoiling that puppy, Thomas. She won't be fit for anything."

Thomas looked down at the puppy, laying on his leg, content after a little venison stew of her own. "I've decided on a name."

"Let's hear it. You've been pondering on that for days."

"I know, but when we first found her, I thought it was a male, and I had a name all picked out. When we got home and saw she was a female, I had to do some thinking."

"Let's hear it, then."

Thomas stroked the puppy's brown velvety ears. "Clementine."

"Perfect."

"I just know Sarah will love her. She loves dogs. And horses, too."

"So what's the whole story here, Thomas? You always talked about Sarah when we were growing up. Then, when you came by here to visit when you moved down to Beaumont to work, you said y'all were finished. Said she married a man she met when he came through Pineville working with the railroad crew."

Thomas rubbed the back of his neck. "She did marry someone else. Nils Andersson. They had two children, Melissa and John." Thomas peered in the distance. "They're the cutest little ones you've ever seen. Anyway, Nils was a Swedish immigrant. He had everything, you know. A wonderful wife, two beautiful children, a nice home. But it wasn't enough. He was homesick. Sarah said he wanted them to go to Sweden, but she felt like the children were too young for a trip like that across the ocean. Well, he decided to go anyway. He left Sarah, Melissa, and John, here, and he took off."

"All this happened while you lived in Beaumont, right?"

"Yes. But I moved back to Pineville after what took place

between me and Watts. I go back home, you know, determined to keep my distance from Sarah, and she and the children are alone because her husband left them to go back for a visit. He never made it back, though. He died in New York."

"Quite a story. I didn't want to ask at first, but I see she's all you think about."

"You're right about that. I fought it for a long time, but I've always been smitten with her."

"I hope it works out this time around."

"So, what about you? Do you plan to live alone up here in the woods?"

Solomon grinned. "I haven't met anyone I'm…uh, how did you put it, smitten with."

"How will you ever meet someone out here?" Thomas gestured to the woods surrounding them.

Solomon sighed. "Enough about me. If we want to do some hunting tomorrow morning we'd better get to sleep."

Thomas leaned his rifle on the door frame then went to the kitchen to find his friend frying up thick slices of the sweet potatoes they had cooked the day before but had not eaten.

"That smells delicious."

Solomon had one iron skillet full of bacon and the other with the sweet potatoes. "I'll cook our eggs in the bacon grease and we can have a hearty breakfast before we get out in the woods. The coffee is dripping but it's not quite ready."

They enjoyed their breakfast but didn't sit long and converse, because the day ahead was full of possibilities. When they moved outside Thomas shivered from the coolness of the early morning.

Solomon breathed in deeply and exhaled. "I think we should go on foot today. We'll ride out on a hunt in a few days. Besides, we can enjoy the beauty of nature more by walking."

"I need to do some walking after that breakfast we just ate. You're a mighty fine cook, Solomon."

"I just cook what my mama always did. I raise what I need and gather berries and nuts off the land. The woods here are really full of all the bounty anyone requires. Squirrels, deer and hogs are all around. Sometimes I get a hankering for a coon or a possum, but not all that often."

Thomas's boot sunk into a bed of leaves. "I think these leaves are four to five inches thick."

"When we pass through a place where hardwoods abound, the leaves are like that. But look, the trees are starting to be green again. And see over there? I thought I smelled some honeysuckle." Solomon closed his eyes. "I'll want to pick some on the way back to the house."

"I think you enjoy just being in the woods more than actually hunting. Am I right?"

"Maybe so."

In an instant Solomon turned and shot behind Thomas, hitting a timber rattler.

Thomas jumped forward and ended up beside Solomon. "How did you see that?"

"I didn't see it. I heard it."

They left the snake lying there, but Thomas didn't want Solomon to know it was the biggest one he had ever seen. It had to be nearly five feet long. He hiked forward but glanced around him. He never heard anything until Solomon shot. Maybe it was time he paid more attention to his surroundings.

They moved on through the forest and came to a clearing leading to the creek. The water glistened in the early sunlight. Cypress trees stood near the bank, their trunks fanned out to a wide base and the roots ran down to meet the creek.

Solomon gazed into the woods. "I thought I saw someone on

horseback over there behind the trees."

Thomas didn't see anything. Solomon cupped his hands and hollered, "Daniel Cain."

The man guided his horse to the creek bank and waved.

"That's Dan Cain. Clark and Thelma's son. I'd know him anywhere."

Solomon motioned for him to come across, and Dan pointed in another direction. "He's crossing below us where it's more shallow. Let's go meet him."

Solomon strode over to join his friend with Thomas following. After Dan and Solomon greeted each other, Solomon introduced Thomas.

Dan Cain nodded. "So you're Thomas Carson."

"Yes, I am. I guess your parents told you I met them."

"No, I'm on my way to their house. They don't even know I'm coming." Dan paused before he spoke again. "I saw a man riding on the road before I came on the path into the thicket. He stopped me and asked if I knew where he could find a Thomas Carson."

A sour taste rose in his mouth. "Did he say his name?"

"I believe his last name was Watts."

Chapter Fourteen

S arah put the finishing touches on the ribbons then placed them around the stems of the dogwoods, honeysuckle and jasmine branches. She had three bouquets to take to the cemetery, so she placed them inside the basket her grandmother always used to transport flowers. The basket was a half bushel in measurement, tightly woven, but made into a rectangle for the purpose of gathering flowers.

She had considered taking the children with her but decided against it. She planned to have the children join her when she did this several times a year, but today she needed to go to the sawmill and do some work after she finished at the cemetery.

She let Eliza know she was leaving and climbed into her wagon and started on her way. She breathed in the delightful scent of the honeysuckle.

There was no sign of Brother Maxwell moving between the church building and the parsonage this morning. Sarah was all ready to stop and visit a minute if she noticed their beloved minister or his wife, Beulah, outside. Their house beside the church showed no signs of movement, so Sarah travelled toward the cemetery.

Before long, she arrived and stopped her wagon near the gate. A horse was tied at the end of the fence. She looked out into the cemetery. A man stood near the graves where her grandfather, grandmother and mother were buried. Sarah turned to leave but he waved, so she decided to take the flowers on out to the graves of

her loved ones.

She didn't recognize him from a distance. It wasn't that awful Mr. Watts, because this man was taller and thinner. And he was well-dressed in his three-piece suit. He looked at her, then he looked down.

She grabbed the basket, let herself into the gate, and strolled toward her family's final resting place. The man stood beside her mother's grave.

She stared at him. Maybe it was someone she knew. But nothing about him was familiar.

Sarah walked over and placed the bouquets on the graves, first on her loving grandfather's, then on her dear grandmother's, and finally on the grave of the mother she loved but did not remember.

The man watched her every move. She extended her hand. "Hello. I'm Sarah Andersson. Do you have loved ones here?"

The man opened his mouth to speak but instead covered his face and wept. Could he be insane? Her heart pounded.

The man gently touched her arm. "I'm so sorry. This is not what I intended." He wiped his tears with his sleeve and studied her face. "Please let me introduce myself. I am Andrew Smith. Your father."

Heat rose in her cheeks. "What a horrible thing to say. My father is dead."

She dropped the basket and ran, pulling her skirt up above her ankles so she could move away from this liar, this man trying to deceive her. But why? Why would someone be so cruel?

She had to get away. What was she thinking, going into the cemetery when she saw the strange man there?

Sarah looked behind her. He still stood in the cemetery beside her mother's grave. At least he wasn't following her.

She headed to town to find Sheriff Walker so he could investigate this stranger. So many things raced through her mind. Did he plan to pretend he was her father and try to get money from her? Did someone tell him she was a young lady, widowed but owning a sawmill and other assets left to her by her grandparents? Well, if this was the plan, he had another thing coming.

Sarah stopped her wagon in front of the sheriff's office and climbed down. She rushed into the building and slammed the door. Sheriff Walker met her at the front of the office.

"I'm so glad you're in. I just left the cemetery." Sarah stopped to catch her breath. "There was a man out there who said he is my father. I have to admit he frightened me. I need you to talk to him."

The sheriff motioned for her to sit in the chair by his desk. "Sarah, had you ever seen him before? Did he give you his name?"

"No, I'd never seen him before. And yes, he said his name is Andrew Smith. That is, or was, my father's name."

"Can you give me a description?"

Sarah closed her eyes for a few seconds. "Yes. He is about Dr. Bailey's height and weight. He has brown hair with some streaks of gray. I think he is in his mid-forties."

Sheriff Walker stood up and pulled on his jacket and hat. "You go on home, Sarah. I'll find him and talk to him. And I'll be over later to tell you what I find out."

"Thank you. I will go home. I have to admit that he made me uneasy."

The sheriff looked around. "My deputy is out checking into another matter. Would you like for me to find someone to escort you home?"

"No, I'll be fine. If you hurry, maybe you can talk to this man and get him out of town."

Sarah scurried out of the office, then stopped on the sidewalk. She looked in every direction for the stranger. When she was satisfied he was not nearby, she started for home. She pictured him sobbing there in the cemetery and shuddered. Who was he and what did he want?

Determined to enjoy the beautiful day once she got home, Sarah took the children outside to play in the backyard. Abigail and Eliza had insisted she go upstairs and rest when she told them what happened, but she wasn't tired. Her muscles still quivered. How could someone come to Pineville and profess to be her father?

No, she surely didn't need to rest. She wanted to stay busy and get her mind off the entire ordeal.

She took a quilt from the blanket chest and spread it on the grass outside. Gus was excited and ran across the quilt more times than she could count. He was a medium sized dog even though he was only a little more than six months old.

The children ran and played chase in the sunshine. In front of the barn Mr. Thompson brushed the horses and hauled water to the troughs so the livestock could drink after munching on their food.

Before long, Abigail ventured out and joined them on the quilt. Then Eliza came and brought freshly baked teacakes for their impromptu picnic.

This was the kind of world Sarah's children should have. Playing alongside their puppy without fear. A world without James Watts or the man at the cemetery. She would try with all her might to give it to them.

When it was time for Uncle Marshall to come home, she waited for him on the porch. He would probably scold her for going out to the cemetery alone, but she'd never had an experience like the one today. How could she have known?

When he walked through the gate, he shook his head. "Sari, I don't know what to make of what happened today. Sheriff Walker came over to the sawmill, and he said he talked to the man you saw at the cemetery. The man insisted on going to see Dr. Bailey, claiming he knew Dr. Bailey years ago."

"What did Dr. Bailey find out about him? Did the sheriff

know?"

"I talked to him again before I came home, and he said Doc does know him and said he will be staying in their home for now. Dr. Bailey assured the sheriff that the man won't contact you."

"That's interesting. But you know I trust Dr. Bailey, so I won't worry. I just wonder if he knew my father in the past, since he knows Dr. Bailey. It was a strange outburst he had, to say the least."

"That's the other thing I was supposed to tell you, Sari. Dr. Bailey told the sheriff he isn't harmful by any means."

Sarah rubbed her forehead. "Maybe not. But the behavior he exhibited wasn't normal. You know I don't exaggerate about such things."

"I know you don't."

Hopefully, this man wouldn't stay in town very long. Perhaps Lucy could shed some light on this friend of Dr. Bailey's. Her chin still trembled when she recalled their meeting. One thing was certain, though. She didn't want to see him again.

Not ever.

Chapter Fifteen

The following day Uncle Marshall arrived home at least an hour later than usual. Sarah may not have noticed if the children had not begun to watch for him so early. After saying only a few words and not explaining his tardiness, he went to the barn to check on things while Abigail and Sarah put supper on the table.

Sarah had not left home the entire day. Even though she tried to dismiss the scene at the cemetery the previous morning as purely unfortunate, the man sobbing and claiming to be her father still caused her to cringe.

Melissa came into the kitchen with John trailing behind her. "Uncle Marshall said he couldn't sit on the porch with us today. He said he had to go out to the barn."

"I'm sorry. Uncle Marshall must have something to do out there. You'll get to spend time with him this evening, I'm sure."

Sarah arranged the fried pork chops on the serving platter. "Abigail, I only want Uncle Marshall to be happy. Don't you think he seems out of sorts this evening? I feel like he's tired of running things at the mill. After I get the children to sleep, I think I'll discuss it with him."

"Charles is supposed to be by tonight after supper. We'll visit in the library if you and Marshall want to discuss this in the parlor. I think it may be a good idea to talk to him about things at the sawmill."

"You know I hoped things would work out so Thomas would be back soon, but he didn't want to seek James Watts out, so he has to wait for the situation to unfold. Of course, he had hoped Mr. Watts may have a change of heart, but after what we saw here, I don't look for it. And, Abigail, I miss him so much and worry every minute about him."

"I'm so sorry all of this came up. I can't imagine how hard it must be on you. But Thomas was wise to move it away from Pineville. You know, maybe this Mr. Watts needs more time to sort things out. Things may look a little different away from prison."

Sarah pulled the cornbread from the oven. "Everything's ready. Could you go and fetch Uncle Marshall? It's so unusual for him to not be in here ready to eat. He's usually the first one to the supper table."

"Sure. He's still out in the barn, I suppose. I'll go tell him we're ready."

Sarah called Melissa and John to wash their hands, then the three of them took their seats at the table. Finally, Abigail and Uncle Marshall made their way into the kitchen.

"Uncle Marshall, can you offer a prayer of thanks for our food?"

He prayed, but he seemed like his mind wasn't on what he said, and that surely wasn't like him. He pushed the food around his plate and ate very little. Abigail glanced at Marshall during the meal, but neither of them made eye contact with her.

She laid her fork beside her plate. "Uncle Marshall, I'd like to visit with you tonight. I'm afraid you're tired of being in charge at the sawmill. I thought Thomas would be back before now. I'm always a little on the optimistic side, you know."

Abigail fixed her gaze on Sarah, then the children. "I would like to help Melissa and John with getting their sleep clothes on and then reading them a story. Could I do that tonight?"

"Sure. I think they'd like that."

With a big smile, Melissa nodded, while John concentrated on getting the peas to his mouth.

As soon as the children finished eating, Sarah began putting the dishes in the pan to soak and Abigail announced she was taking the children upstairs.

Her uncle waited until he and Sarah were alone in the kitchen before he began a conversation. "Sari, we need to go to the parlor and talk."

"Let me finish here. I know you're tired of being in charge at the mill. I'd like to mention some men to you who may be able to manage things for a week or two. That way you can go by the mill if you'd like to, or you and Abigail can spend time at your property."

"This is not about the mill. It's something far more important. I need you to come with me to the parlor now."

She dried her hands on the dish towel and followed her uncle. Was he ill? Had something happened to Thomas?

Sarah took her place in the chair by her desk where she always sat. Uncle Marshall settled in to the armchair.

"I need to break some news to you."

Her heart was in her throat. "Is it Thomas? Has something happened? Oh, Uncle Marshall, I can't lose him."

"I haven't heard from Thomas. As far as everybody knows, he's doin' well. The thing is, you're not losing anyone. But you are gaining someone." His eyes glistened with tears.

"What do you mean? Tell me."

"I can't beat around the bush any longer. The man you saw at the cemetery is your father."

The room swayed. "What did you say?"

She stood and wrung her hands. "No, that's not true."

Uncle Marshall wiped his forehead with his sleeve. "Dr. Bailey sent for me today. I went to his office and he had Andrew there." He stared down at the floor. "I know him, Sari. Dr. Bailey knows him."

"He's not my father." Sarah curled her lip. "If he's my father, where has he been all these years?"

"He says he's very sorry for not being here."

She bolted from the parlor and up the stairs. She held her tears until she could make it to the balcony outside her bedroom. Then she sobbed, just the way the man at the cemetery had sobbed.

Chapter Sixteen

Thomas and Clementine meandered along the trail. How long could the puppy scurry around on those little legs? After spending a few days in the woods with Solomon, Thomas could navigate the trails around him pretty well, so while Solomon made one of his bi-yearly trips to town, he and Clementine would venture out on their own.

How Thomas had prayed that Watts would lose the evil thoughts of seeking vengeance and move along. But Dan Cain confirmed Watts had not had a change of heart.

Bothering him almost more than Watts was the fact he had been gone too long from home. He closed his eyes and allowed visions of Sarah to skirt across his mind. Maybe it had been foolish to leave town, but it surely wasn't wise for the problems he faced due to his past to be showcased in his hometown. His greatest fear was that if he stayed in Pineville and Sarah and the children got hurt, or maybe even other innocent people, he could never forgive himself.

Out here, he could finally face James Watts without fear of anyone else being injured. And he had to convince Solomon to stay out of the way if Watts came for him.

A sizeable hickory log lay on the ground between a thick growth of hardwoods and bushes, the perfect place for Clementine to rest. This spot would also give him a quiet place to take time to think. He was getting a little weary of not having a normal life—a life where he had responsibilities and relationships. How did

Solomon exist in such a solitary way?

Thomas laid back on the log. He gazed at the sky, void of clouds. The tall green pines against the blue sky was like a painted mural to savor. And savor he would.

Of course, any quiet time became time to think about Sarah. His days were not complete without seeing her and touching that light brown hair, peering into her green, green eyes and feeling the softness of his lips against hers.

Maybe he should go and get Blaze from Solomon's place and just ride through the woods and river bottom searching for Watts. Just so this waiting game could be over, once and for all. But then, he would be the aggressor. And that was not his style.

No, he would wait and pray for a plan to stop the hate-and-vengeance-filled scheme of James Watts.

Soft snoring sounds came from Clementine napping on the grass below him. The walk this morning had been a long one for her. He may have to carry her part of the way home.

The birds were the only sound in the forest this morning, especially the chirping of the small buntings, ushering in spring. At times like this, Thomas understood why Solomon loved it out here. The thicket was a great place to find solitude and reconnect with the desires of his heart. But no place was the perfect one without the love of his life. And Thomas had to grin, thinking of Sarah ever living way out here.

No, she loved being with people, and she loved her grandparent's home, the sawmill her grandfather established, and Pineville. She often said she wanted her children to grow up there, like she did.

The distinctive crunching of tree limbs spread on the floor of the forest reached him. Thomas lifted his head to look for the cause of the sound he heard. He eased from the log to lay beside Clementine, behind the bushes and brush.

A horse with a rider appeared. The profile of the rider made him blink twice. It had to be James Watts. He surely favored his brother.

He rode past Thomas, never looking his way. So Watts was close. Or maybe he was passing through the thicket, planning to ride the length of it. Only time would tell.

Thomas lay motionless for a while after Watts moved on. After a while, he was safe to head back to Solomon's place, so he picked up a still sleeping Clementine and hit the trail. It had been good to see James Watts from a distance and get a look at the buckskin horse he rode. Now he had seen him with his own eyes, and the time was drawing near for them to cross paths.

He glanced over his shoulder again and again while he walked, trying to make sure he wasn't being followed. Clementine was still content being carried along. Thankfully, she had not uttered her sharp little barks.

Before he reached the house, rain came pelting down, so he slipped Clementine under his shirt. He couldn't wait to show his puppy to Sarah and the children. Like he did every day, he hoped he would be heading home soon. And when he headed home, he wanted James Watts to be heading out somewhere, too. That was his prayer.

Chapter Seventeen

When Sarah opened her eyes to the sunlight streaming through her window, she sat up in bed and yawned. She laid back on the puffy feather pillow again. Then she covered her head with the quilt.

Why did this have to happen to me? I'm already worried sick about Thomas. Now this man wants me to welcome him as my father?

She had two choices this morning. Stay in bed all day and claim to be sick or get out of bed and try to proceed with the matters at hand. She definitely needed to be at the office at the mill today. There were too many people counting on her, so she had to proceed with the matters at hand.

When she heard a light tap on the bedroom door, she uncovered her head. "Who is it?"

"Abigail, dear."

"Come in."

Abigail entered the room with a tray laden with breakfast, including pancakes, cane syrup and bacon. Then in one corner was a cup of steaming coffee and in the other a delicate vase with a stem of a flowering redbud. Sarah smiled at the beautiful pink blooms and decided right then and there she would make this day a productive one.

"Oh, Abigail, you are so thoughtful and just plain sweet."

"Marshall and I want you to know we are here for you. We'll

do anything we can to help you through this situation."

"And what a situation it is. I know everyone, including Mr. Andrew Smith, thinks I should be happy to see him, but I'm not. I don't even know this man."

Sarah reached for the coffee. "I suppose you cooked this breakfast since Eliza is not here yet." She took a sip. "Umm. A few minutes ago I didn't know if I would even get out of bed today. I appreciate this so much."

"I think you need time to get used to the fact that your father is indeed alive. Even though you feel such disdain for him, and we understand that, give it some time. Don't do anything you'll regret later."

Sarah poured the cane syrup over the pancakes. "Won't you eat some of this with me?"

"Thanks, but I ate with Marshall before he left for the mill." Abigail pulled the stool from Sarah's dressing table beside the bed. "I'll sit here with you if you don't mind."

"I don't mind. I never mind if you and Marshall are with me. But I don't want to see this Mr. Smith. That's what I've decided." Sarah cut the crisp bacon with her fork and put it up to her mouth. "I don't have much for a man who deserts his child."

After Sarah ate most of the breakfast Abigail prepared for her, Sarah poured water from the pitcher into the bowl on her dresser and washed her face. When Eliza arrived, she planned to head to the saw mill. Abigail would care for the children until Eliza came, but she didn't want to impose. They did enough for her and the children already.

Oh, how she wished Thomas could be with her now. She missed him so much every day and she had not heard from him since the gift of the honey appeared on the porch. Why, something terrible could have happened and she may not even realize it yet. Sarah closed her eyes and shook her head. She would not let those thoughts invade her mind this morning.

Why does this all have to happen now? Why couldn't this Andrew Smith have shown up when she had Thomas safe at home in Pineville?

Yes, if Thomas were here, he would pull her close and assure her that he understood her feelings. He would not expect her to suddenly accept this stranger into her life.

Sarah pulled a printed skirt and a white cotton shirtwaist from the chifforobe. Even though the small buttons ran down the length of the back of the blouse, Abigail or Eliza would button them for her.

Once Sarah was dressed and making her way downstairs to ask for help with the buttons on her blouse, she discovered her friend, Lucy Bailey, sitting in the kitchen with Abigail.

"Lucy, what a surprise. What brings you out so early this morning?"

Lucy ran to Sarah and hugged her. "I wanted to visit with you. We haven't been able to talk much lately."

"Sure. I'd love to visit. We can do just that while you attempt to button this blouse."

Abigail pushed her chair back and stood up. "If you ladies will excuse me, I think I'll check on the children."

Lucy pushed Sarah's hair to the side and worked on the buttons. "Have you heard from Thomas?"

"Not this week. Last week someone delivered a crock container with fresh honey inside. It had my name on it in Thomas's handwriting, so I knew it was from him, and I felt so relieved to know he was all right."

Lucy patted Sarah's back. "All done. Could we sit for a moment?"

"Sure. I'm not leaving for the sawmill until Eliza gets here."

Lucy took a deep breath. "You know your father, well uh, Dr. Smith, is staying in our home. And I wanted to tell you how kind he is, and he is so hopeful..."

Heat flushed through her entire body. Her face had to be a crimson color by now. "Hopeful? Hopeful that I will allow him to be a part of my life when it's convenient for him?" Sarah shook her head. "You have no idea what this is like, Lucy. Your father has always been there for you. Been there to tuck you in at night, walk you to school, sit by you in church. I don't even want to talk to this Andrew Smith."

Sarah studied Lucy's face. "Did he ask you to come here and talk to me? Well, you can tell him I don't want to see him. He needs to stay out of my way."

"He didn't ask me to come. I just felt like I should talk to you and tell you what kind of person he is. Maybe you need time to think about this."

Just then Eliza knocked lightly on the door and entered the kitchen. "Good mornin'."

"Good morning, come on in." Sarah stood and pushed her chair under the table.

"I'd better get on down to the mill. While Thomas is away, I really have to look over and approve the orders and expenses."

"I know you do. I won't detain you. We can talk more later." Lucy patted Eliza on the arm. "So good to see you. I hope your family is doing well."

"Yes, they are. Good to see you too, Miss Lucy."

Once Lucy left, Eliza hugged Sarah. "I heard the news. My cousin works for Mrs. Bailey, and she said your daddy is a really nice man."

"I'm sure he is. But I don't know him." Sarah clasped her hands in front of her. "Oh, and he's not allowed here to see the children. Understand?"

"Yes, I understand."

Sarah walked out the back door and motioned for Mr. Thompson to bring the wagon around. She had work to do at the office. She didn't have time to spend worrying about this Andrew

Smith. Besides, she had lived twenty-two years without a father. What was the rush now?

Chapter Eighteen

Sarah stared straight ahead when she moved her wagon through town. The news about Andrew had to be circulating. She knew all too well what the townspeople were looking for. Slightly red or swollen eyes or her not being as talkative as normal were things that could surely get the whispers started. There wasn't much happening in this tiny town, so the talk would center around her situation until something else newsworthy came along.

Since she didn't stop at Wright's Mercantile, the post office, or visit with anyone along the way, she arrived at the mill to begin her work much earlier than usual. And as a result, she walked into the office to hear Clyde Morgan quizzing her Uncle Marshall. "So, you all thought he was dead until now? Where has he been all this time?"

When the door closed behind her, the conversation ended, and both men greeted her.

"Glad to see you, Mrs. Andersson. I have some orders for you to approve and some invoices I need to pay."

Sarah moved to the door of her private office and turned the knob. "If they're on my desk I'll look at them right away. I'll be here most of the day, Mr. Morgan."

When she was settled in at her desk, Uncle Marshall came into her office. "Mind if I sit down?"

"You know you're welcome any time."

"Sari, about last night. I had to be the one to tell you, and I want you to know I wasn't expecting you to be happy about it. It was a shock to all of us." He shook his head. "I'm puzzled about the whole thing."

"I don't blame you. It's just that I can't embrace the idea of a father when he's never been around. He was an emotional wreck at the cemetery the day he told me who he was. If and when I do talk to him, I hope he's more composed."

"It's strange, for sure. I don't know all the details. I just know we were told years ago that he died and that was that. They buried him over in San Jacinto County somewhere, they said. Your mother had already passed on, and Albert went and brought her home to be buried here in Pineville. The day your grandfather traveled over there, Andrew was sick with the fever, and the doctor that was there said he was quarantined."

Sarah gazed out the window. "So, he really didn't die. I don't know how that news was spread. But he knew where to find me. He knew I was here, and he never came. That is, until now."

"I'm mighty sorry, Sari."

"Well, don't you worry. The shock of it all upset me last night, but I'm better today. I don't plan to see him right now." Sarah raised her chin. "And I mean that. If I ever feel the need to talk to him, I'll let him know."

"It's up to you. Me and Abigail will help you however we can." Uncle Marshall smoothed his hair into place. "I just hope we can get Tom back home."

"So you are tired of running the saw mill." When she glanced her uncle's way, Sarah chuckled.

"We all know it's not my favorite thing to do, but I mostly just miss that boy. And I know you and those young'uns do too."

"Yes, we do. I miss him, but I want him to handle Mr. Watts how he sees fit. I'm so thankful he's with his friend, Solomon. I don't know him, but Thomas has great respect for him. It's helps to know Thomas isn't all alone in the thicket."

Uncle Marshall turned to leave. "I'll let you get to work."

"Thanks for everything."

Work at the office kept her occupied and her mind off this Mr. Smith. She pored over the invoices and orders Mr. Morgan brought to her. When she heard a knock at her office door, she had to glance at the clock, because she had barely looked up once she started to work. Sarah was amazed to find it was already 10:45.

"Who is it?'

"It's Dr. Bailey. May I come in?"

Sarah rose from the chair and walked to the door. She didn't want to ask him to come in for fear he may have his friend, Andrew Smith, with him.

She opened the door just enough to see if he was alone. "Come in."

Dr. Bailey pulled Sarah close and hugged her. "I really need to talk with you for a few minutes. I hope this is a good time."

"Yes, it's a really good time. I want to talk with you, too, and I'd rather not do it at my home when the children are around." Sarah sat behind her desk and motioned for Dr. Bailey to take one of the chairs in front of her.

"I'll get right to the point. Andrew is an old friend of mine. I truly thought he was deceased." Dr. Bailey nodded. "I would have never lied to you about this. I want you to know this first and foremost. When he showed up at my office, it was a shock to me, for sure."

"I'm not blaming you. But you must imagine how this has made me feel. I don't remember him, because I was only two years old when he was supposed to have died. And I've lived all these years thinking he was dead, when all along he had abandoned me."

"He plans to stay in Pineville for a while. He'll begin staying at the hotel today. You see, he knows this is not easy for you, but he wants to make amends and tell you why this all happened."

Sarah sighed. "I'd prefer that he leave and go back where he came from. Just tell him that I don't want to talk right now, and I'll let him know if I ever decide to."

Dr. Bailey made his way to the door. "I have patients waiting, so I need to get back. I'll tell him I spoke with you. Don't worry, he won't cause trouble for you. He's not that kind of man."

"Do you really know what kind of man he is? You haven't seen him for years."

"Yes, I do. He's a fine man who has made a big, big, mistake. And now he wants to correct it, no matter how long it takes."

Exhaustion overwhelmed Sarah when Dr. Bailey left her office. How could everyone overlook her father's absence all these years? And why did this Mr. Smith think he had the right to stay in Pineville?

She gathered the paperwork she had done that morning and headed to Mr. Morgan's office. He was not at his desk. He had probably gone to lunch. She put the things he had requested she approve on his desk.

She had planned to stay all day at the office, but now she wanted to get back home. After Melissa and John finished their afternoon nap the three of them would walk down to the creek and sit on the bank. And maybe, just maybe, it would be warm enough to put their toes in the water and let the cares of the world float away.

Chapter Nineteen

Thomas and Solomon finished the chores around the place and sat on the back porch and enjoyed the perfect morning. They had a full view of the beautiful white dogwoods blooming between the hardwoods, redbud trees with an array of pink flowers, and yellow jasmine trailing among the smaller trees.

"You know, Solomon, I've never seen so many things blooming at one time in one place."

"Oh, it's a show, all right. I love to be in the middle of it out here." Solomon closed his eyes and inhaled. "That honeysuckle over by the barn is as fragrant as a fine perfume."

Thomas removed his hat and put it on the chair beside him. "Yes it is. But I feel plumb lazy just sitting here."

"Our work is all done. I thought we'd fry some fish up in a little bit. That is after we go check our lines."

"Sounds like a good idea."

"You know, I'm thinking you may be perfect for this life. All this huntin' and fishin' in the big woods seems to agree with you."

Thomas swatted at a mosquito that buzzed around his head. "I've enjoyed your hospitality for sure. And I have to admit that the time has passed pretty quickly with all our adventures, but I miss Sarah something awful. If I could leave this minute and head back to Pineville, I'd do it."

"I have to say I'm kind of jealous of you. I've never known love like that." Solomon pulled out his pocket knife and scraped around his thumbnail. "Maybe I'd be better off if I didn't."

"No sir. If you ever meet a woman that makes you feel like this, you'd better latch on to her. There's nothing else like it."

Clementine's ears perked up, and she stared into the clearing. "What do you hear, girl?"

Solomon chuckled. "I'll bet it's Mr. Cain riding over for a visit. He comes in the back way."

"Back way? I didn't know there was such a thing."

"We have our secrets. You know, trails we don't want other folks to find out about."

Thomas reached over and played like he was punching his friend. "Oh, you mean folks like me."

"No. I mean folks like this Watts fellow."

Thomas heart pounded. "You don't think that's Watts, do you?"

"No, it's not an easy trail to find. You have to know it's there."

Just then Clark Cain emerged from the woods and waved to them.

"There he is. Just like I predicted." Solomon moved off the porch to greet him. "Come on up and sit a spell."

Clark let his horse in the lot and lumbered up to the porch. "Before I forget, Mrs. Cain sent y'all some of her teacakes. She makes the best."

"That is a fact." Solomon reached for the pouch. "I'll make some coffee, and we'll let Thomas sample them."

Mr. Cain sat on Solomon's chair with the cowhide bottom. "I'll take a cup of water first if you'll get me some." Solomon eased over to the gourd dipper and poured some water in a cup.

He took a drink then settled back in his chair. "I don't want you boys to get too comfortable now. I had a visitor up at my place yesterday." Mr. Cain turned to face Thomas. "He was looking for the man that killed his brother."

"Wait a minute. Thomas, tell him the story. Tell him how his brother came after you with a knife and you weren't even armed."

Mr. Cain reached to free his pants leg from the top of his boot. "I figured so much. A few minutes with that feller told me what I needed to know about him. But he's close by, camping out by the river. So, be careful."

Thomas rubbed his forehead. "I saw him from a distance the other day, riding along not too far from the creek. I'm ready to end this and get back home, but I don't know exactly what to do yet. I would love to talk to him and make him see what happened."

"After visiting with him yesterday, I don't think that'll help. Won't amount to a hill of beans with that feller."

"I guess we need to make a plan of some kind. We've been waiting to see how things played out, but he's a little too close for comfort now."

Mr. Cain wiped perspiration from his brow. "No, I think you need to give it some time. Give him a little rope, and he might hang himself."

Thomas nodded. How much time did he have? He couldn't wait much longer to be with Sarah. Or could he? If he made the wrong move now, then where would Sarah and the children be? He wet his lips. Mr. Cain was right. He had to give it a little more time. There was no other way around it.

Chapter Twenty

Before she walked into Wright's Mercantile, Sarah straightened her skirt. She had forgotten the list Eliza had given her this morning, so she would do her best, and maybe she could remember some of the things needed at home.

After she greeted Walter Wright behind the counter, she put her mind to gathering the household items Eliza had requested. She had finished earlier than expected at the sawmill, so she looked forward to spending time outside with Melissa and John once she got home. But first, she had to try to remember the items Eliza had asked her to get.

Coffee beans were on the list. Now if she could just remember the other items. Did Eliza also need flour, or was it sugar?

The bell on the front door jingled, signaling a customer entering the store. Mr. Wright issued a stifled greeting. Perhaps it was a stranger or a customer he wasn't particularly fond of.

She turned to see who entered the store. Sarah's heart skipped a beat when her eyes landed on Andrew Smith. She made a beeline for the back of the store and settled between a bolt of checked gingham and a bolt of blue organza.

After what seemed an eternity, Mr. Wright asked Mr. Smith if he could help him find what he needed. Then she heard Mr. Smith's voice and she listened to his reply. He spoke softly but she thought he said he would come back later. Then he thanked Mr. Wright.

Sarah stayed behind the fabric until she heard the bell on the door. Her father's voice was much different than that day in the cemetery. Pleasant. Almost melodic.

She didn't care, though. Lots of people had a nice voice. Why even an outlaw could have a good voice. Was a man who abandoned his child any better than an outlaw?

What was the verse from First Timothy that her grandmother used to recite? *"But if any provide not for his own, and specially for those of his own house, he hath denied the faith, and is worse than an infidel."*

Grandmother surely had no tolerance for a man who didn't take care of his family. And her grandfather had even less tolerance, if that was possible. What would they think now about her father?

Sarah made her way to the front of the store. "I forgot my list at home, Mr. Wright. I think I'll come back tomorrow."

"Sure Mrs. Andersson. Good day."

As soon as she stepped onto the sidewalk Sarah exhaled. She didn't glance around for fear she may see him, lurking. Once she had climbed into the wagon she headed toward home.

How could she make him leave? He had no right to be here. Her grandfather started this town when he built the sawmill. There was no place for her father here.

She loved her name when she was growing up. *Sarah Elizabeth Smith.* Little did she know that Andrew Smith was alive and not caring about her one bit. She had a vivid mental image of her parents and her together when she was small. They would have been similar to Lucy Bailey's folks. She understood hers couldn't be with her, because they had become ill and passed from this life. With the help of her grandparents, she was at peace with her lot in life.

But now her father tainted that vision. She could only picture her mother holding her as a child, smoothing her hair, soothing her when she cried. Beaming at her first word, first steps. There was no father in the vision of her happy little family before she came to live with her grandparents.

If only Thomas were here to see this very strange chapter in her life. How long would it take to settle things with James Watts? But he didn't just want to settle things with Watts. Thomas wanted to try to make him understand that he didn't intend to take his brother's life.

Thomas had been gone for one month. She had endured thirty days of missing him, worrying over his very existence, and fearing for his life. Oh, how she yearned to hear his voice and feel his hand in hers. But all she could do was wait. And that was her least favorite thing to do.

Chapter Twenty-One

S arah held the combs in her hand. Before she placed them in her hair, she always studied them for a few moments, imagining her mother choosing them. This particular set was Sarah's favorite—tortoise shell combs with rhinestones on each one in the shape of a flower. Her grandmother had been wise to save them for her until she was old enough to value them. Her grandmother was the wisest woman she ever knew.

Had her grandparents ever discovered her father was actually alive and chose not to tell her? Surely not. They weren't the kind of people to keep something like that from her when she became an adult. No. They must not have known.

Sarah headed to the children's room to wake them and dress them for church. As she made her way down the hall, they were talking in the bedroom.

"You'd better wake up, John. Maybe we can see Uncle Marshall before he goes to work and tell him we want to go fishing."

Sarah entered the room just as John rubbed his eyes and shook his head while his sister stood beside the bed.

"Good morning. I'm afraid there won't be any fishing this morning. It's Sunday. After breakfast, we'll leave for church with Uncle Marshall and Aunt Abigail."

The children's clothes still lay on the chair where she set them the night before. "Melissa, come over and let me wash your face so we can get your clothes on. This may be the last time you get to wear this pink brocade. We're into April and the long sleeves will begin to be too warm."

She had better dress Melissa while John was slowly gathering energy for the day. Where had the time gone? It wouldn't be long until their summer birthdays would come around, and Melissa would be five and John three.

In the coming months, she would talk to them about their own father. Then when they were older, she could share the letter from the kind police sergeant in New York who had notified her of Nils's death. She would assure them that their father had died in a noble way, saving two children from a fire in a tenement in New York.

But mostly they needed to know how much he loved both of them, even though he felt like he needed to visit his home in Sweden. Thomas would be a wonderful, loving father to the children, but she wanted them to know they had been twice blessed, beginning with the love of their own father. Just like she always believed that she was, because her grandfather filled the role of her father. And now that she realized her own father had deserted her, perhaps she wasn't twice blessed after all.

While she brushed Melissa's hair, she heard footsteps on the landing at the top of the stairs. With a soft knock on the door to the children's room, Abigail came in to check and see if she needed any assistance.

"Come in. One is nearly finished and one more to go."

"Well, don't you girls look nice?" Abigail's smile always brightened the entire room. It certainly competed with the sun streaming through the organza curtains this morning.

"Thank you. And you look beautiful, Abigail."

After Abigail thanked Sarah she went to sit beside John. "Would you like some of Aunt Abigail's pancakes this morning?"

John sat up in bed, nodding.

"Well, let's get you dressed, and we can all go downstairs and have some breakfast."

"Has Uncle Marshall waited until now to have breakfast?"

"No. I cooked for him before I ever dressed. I waited to eat breakfast with the three of you. He's outside in the barn harnessing the team since Mr. Earl is off today."

"Somehow I knew he wouldn't be sitting around the kitchen table."

Before long they were downstairs and had finished the fluffy pancakes with cane syrup, fresh butter, and sausage links and bacon Abigail had prepared.

Uncle Marshall sauntered into the kitchen as they finished eating. "Who is ready to go to church?"

John jumped from his chair to run to Uncle Marshall. Melissa rose from her chair slowly, as though she didn't want to wrinkle her dress or mess up her hair.

"Wait a minute. Let's wash our hands and probably our faces, too. I'm sure I saw syrup on both of you just now." Sarah grabbed a cloth and headed to the washbowl and pitcher by the sink. With a few swipes, they were clean once more.

"I just remembered I left my Bible in the children's room. If y'all can put Melissa and John in the wagon, I'll be right down."

She retrieved her Bible from the table beside Melissa's bed where she left it and headed down to the entry way. Just as she reached the bottom of the stairs Melissa asked, "Where is Mr. Thomas, Uncle Marshall?"

"He had to go on a trip. But we look for him back here any time now."

Melissa nodded. Hopefully, he was right. "Any time now" really wasn't soon enough, though. She needed to see him sooner. *The sooner the better.*

At the church building Dr. and Mrs. Bailey walked up the steps with Lucy behind them. Andrew Smith wasn't anywhere in sight. Sarah exhaled a breath she didn't even know she had been holding. Perhaps he had given up and left town. How Sarah wished that was true.

Once they were inside, Lucy came over to her. "I've missed seeing you. Do you mind if I come visit one day this week?"

"No, I'd love to see you and I know the children would, too." Sarah felt heat rise in her cheeks. "But Lucy, I don't want to discuss Andrew."

"I have no intentions of discussing that subject. I don't want to lose a friend over problems that aren't really mine."

Sarah touched Lucy's arm. "You'll never lose this friend. Come by one afternoon. I have to spend almost every morning at the sawmill."

"Any word from Thomas?"

Sarah shook her head. "Not in several weeks. I pray he will be home soon."

The buzz of conversation in the church quietened. She barely made it to their pew before Mr. Wright walked to the front of the congregation with his song book.

They made it through three songs before Melissa motioned that she needed to go outdoors to the privy. She grabbed her daughter's hand, and they walked toward the back door. Sarah returned the smiles of the other church members as they strolled down the aisle, until her eyes landed on Andrew Smith. He sat on the last pew alone. Her smile faded and she released Melissa's hand. He bowed his head and brushed away a tear.

She couldn't pretend to like him. It wasn't that she had no feelings for him. The problem was she disliked him immensely.

Once they were outside, Melissa stopped and looked at Sarah. "Mama, what's wrong?"

"I'm not feeling well. We'll not go back in the church house.

It's a beautiful day, and Uncle Marshall and Aunt Abigail will look after John."

Sarah eyed a bench that was used when they had a dinner on the grounds. "When we come back from the privy, we'll sit on this bench until the services end. Now let's go."

When they returned, they took their seat. The squirrels chattered while they ran up the trees then chased each other down again. Finally, the doors to the church were propped open, and the people began filing outside.

Lucy Bailey exited and looked all around, then headed in their direction. "I was worried when y'all didn't come back in. What happened?"

Melissa jumped up. "Mama is sick."

Lucy sat beside Sarah. "What is wrong, Sarah?"

"I'm not feeling well, that's all. As soon as Uncle Marshall and Abigail come out with John, we'll go home."

"I hope you feel better."

Sarah kept her attention on Brother Maxwell as he talked with Andrew. A wave of nausea passed over her when Beulah Maxwell guided him toward their house next door to the church. Brother Maxwell made his way over to her.

"Hello, Sarah. I was concerned when you and Melissa didn't come back in earlier. Are you both feeling all right?"

"I don't feel well but I'll be better soon."

"Could I talk with you for a moment?"

Lucy took Melissa by the hand. "Let's find your Uncle Marshall."

Sarah stood up and guided Melissa back to her side. "That won't be necessary. Melissa will stay with me."

Sarah smiled reassuringly at her daughter. "Brother Maxwell, we can talk some other time, I'm sure."

"Yes, we can. But I'd like to visit with you soon. Good day, Sarah. And goodbye to you, Melissa."

She headed toward their wagon with Melissa beside her. Once they took their seats, Uncle Marshall sauntered over and placed John beside her.

Abigail finished her conversation with her son and hurried over to the wagon. Uncle Marshall helped her up to her seat and clucked to the horses. Sarah noticed her uncle moved along without speaking for a few minutes. When he finally spoke, he had a gruffness to his voice. "Dr. Bailey wants you to meet him at his office this afternoon. I told him I'd tell you, but I couldn't promise you'd be there."

She sighed. "I'll go. Only because I want to put an end to this, here and now. Everyone wants to help, and no one knows what to do, except me. I'm really weary of it all."

The others chatted, but Sarah closed her eyes and let go of the vision of her father she had held on to all these years. He had been a handsome, protective figure in her mind. The form fluttered away, and she and her mother stood all alone.

Chapter Twenty-Two

Thomas saddled Blaze and stroked his mane. Enoch, Solomon's black mouth cur, stood close by, yelping, then turning in circles, ready for the hunt. But Clementine was to stay behind. Solomon thought he was too protective of the puppy and he probably was. But he longed for the day he could return home with her in tow, and he wasn't taking any chances on her getting lost or hurt somehow. Sarah and the children would love her as much as he did. Hopefully Gus, Melissa and John's dog, approved of her.

Perspiration formed along his hairline. The warmer days were upon them, and the cool, early spring mornings were probably going to be few and far between now.

How much longer would he be here in the thicket? His patience was wearing thin, and he had to get home soon. He had prayed again this morning that God would show him how to resolve this situation in the best way for everyone.

Was Watts still out here? He figured he could have gotten tired of being in the thicket and just left. Maybe Watts thought finding Thomas was kind of like a needle in a haystack. Or maybe he was determined to seek revenge regardless of the time it may take.

Thomas didn't want the possibility of trouble hanging over his head—the threat of Watts showing up later in Pineville, causing problems. He truly wanted to face it now. Get it over with.

But he had gone over and over it in his mind, tossing and turning in his bed most nights, remembering the horror he felt when he realized he had taken the life of another human being. "Thou shalt not kill". Exodus chapter twenty, verse thirteen was etched in his mind. Thomas did not want to be in that situation again, defending himself, fighting to the end.

Solomon finally marched out of the house, blowing horn strapped across his chest. Time for the hunt. Maybe today he would hunt more than deer or hogs. Maybe it was time to do a little hunting for James Watts and just see if he could convince him to settle the situation peacefully.

Solomon tossed him a horn. "Here's one for you in case we get separated."

Thomas turned it over in his hand. "This is a nice one. Should I practice first? You know, to get the feel of it?"

"Naw. That one belonged to me when I was younger, so I'd know the sound even if you didn't blow it worth a darn. The one I use now belonged to my father. He made it from a big steer's horn and later covered it with skin from the leg of a deer."

"I know you treasure the one that belonged to your father. Thanks for letting me use yours. I appreciate it."

Solomon laid his rifle on his shoulder. "We'd better be going. Perfect day for hunting."

Thomas planted his foot in the stirrup and swung his other leg over Blaze's back. "I need to look for Watts today. It's been nice being here with you but I'm ready to get back home." He rested his rifle between him and the saddle horn. "I can't stand to be away from Sarah any longer. It's wearing on me now. And I need to get back and help her at the mill."

"Your life sounds exhausting. You're in love. You run a sawmill. Those are complicated things." Solomon grinned and nodded.

"Being in love isn't always complicated. It's…oh, well. You'll see someday."

"Yeah. When someone comes in the thick of these woods and

finds me."

Thomas twisted in the saddle to take a look around. "Where are we headed? I still don't know my way around here like I should."

"We're headed to the creek. Things may look more familiar in a few minutes." Solomon lowered his voice a little. "Are you serious about looking for Watts?"

"Yes, I am. I thought he'd come up to your place by now or hide and wait for me on the trail. It's gone on way too long."

"He's supposed to be camping down by the river, according to Mr. Cain." Solomon chuckled. "He might be lost in the woods. Who knows?"

Before long they were in thicker brush and on the trail of a buck. The deer were plentiful in the thicket, but Solomon liked to work a little for his fresh meat. Otherwise he would have walked a few feet from his house and brought home plenty for them to feast on.

When they stopped to eat and rest a bit, Solomon led them to a scenic spot on the creek bank. The horses drank and grazed while the hunters pulled their provisions from their leather knapsacks.

"I see why you love it out here, Solomon. I hope I can bring John out here in a few years to see how a woodsman lives."

"I'd like that. So, you think things will work out for you and this Sarah to marry."

"Yes, I do. In fact, when I get back home, I'm asking her to marry me as soon as we can get a wedding together. She wanted to wait until her husband's been gone for a year, but I've decided it's time. Those two children need a father and well, Sarah may not think she needs a husband, but I know she loves me."

"I can't wait to meet this woman. She sounds like an independent one."

Thomas smiled. "She's independent. Smart. Kind. And beautiful."

"Sounds like she's out of your reach."

Thomas picked up a rock to toss at his friend, but he dropped it when they heard three long blows from a horn. Solomon turned and frowned. "I don't recognize that horn." He immediately put his horn to his mouth and blew two long signals.

"Is that what I think it is?" Thomas's narrowed his eyes.

"Yep, it is. Three long blows mean 'come to me'. Two long blows like I just did mean 'we're on our way'." Solomon rose from his resting place on the log and gathered the food and his knapsack.

"Let's get going. I don't know who it is, but somebody needs help. They may be lost, since I didn't recognize the sound." Solomon rubbed his beard. "Out here we all know how each blowing horn sounds and who owns it. I'm curious now to see who we'll find."

Thomas and Solomon were on the trail in no time. The horn blew again as they rode, but the last one of the three faded.

Solomon shouted, "We'd better pick up the pace. That sure don't sound good."

When they came to a slough Enoch barked and ran toward some downed trees. Only then did they see a man lying on his back on the ground, moaning. His horse stood about twenty feet away.

Solomon reined his horse in and ran to the man's side.

Thomas sat frozen for a few seconds. The horse resembled the buckskin he saw Watts riding the day he observed him from afar. The man lifted his head and stared their way. The dark steely eyes, coarse brown hair. Without a doubt it was him.

His pulse raced. Thomas stopped Blaze right there and eased down until his feet were steady. Should he move closer or was this a ploy?

James Watts lowered his head. "Can you help me?"

Solomon kneeled beside him. "What happened?"

Watts glanced at Thomas then looked back again at Solomon. "I was riding along, and my horse stammered. I thought it was because he didn't want to step over a couple of these downed trees. So I nudged him with my spur and when I did, he rared up. While I was on my way to the ground, I saw a rattlesnake. That's what spooked him." He rubbed his leg. "I hit my leg on this log. But worse than that, the snake bit me on my arm, clean through my shirt."

Solomon winced. "Timber rattler. They can strike through your clothes or even a leather boot."

"I can't move. If y'all hadn't come I would lay right here and die."

Solomon motioned to Thomas. "Come give me a hand."

Thomas inched toward the injured man. "Watts, do you have a gun on you?"

"I know who you are, Carson. I've been aching to see you, but not this way."

Solomon walked back to Thomas, his posture stiffening. "Your call. What do we do?"

"Make sure he's not armed or doesn't have a trick up his sleeve."

Solomon ran his hands along Watts's body checking for weapons. "I know you're not out here without something besides that rifle on your saddle."

"There's a buck knife in the scabbard on my saddle."

Solomon stood, still facing Watts. "Thomas, like I said, it's your call."

Thomas moved closer. "Is his leg broken?"

"I think it is. He can't move it without a lot of pain."

"Let's give him some help. That's the right thing to do."

"I thought you'd say that." Solomon returned to the injured man's side.

By now, James Watts' face had broken out in a sweat. "My leg is paining me, but I'm worried about this snake bite. It was a big rattlesnake."

Thomas stood beside Watts. "I have no intention to bring you harm, just as I didn't plan to harm your brother. We'll help you the best we can."

Watts's voice cracked. "I'm...I'm much obliged."

Solomon grabbed his knife from the scabbard and cut the shirt sleeve away above the snake bite. He then tied a piece of cloth above the wound.

"If you'll cut about a quarter of an inch into these fang marks, I'll try to suck the poison out."

"All right. Let me get the water I put in my canteen when we stopped back there. It'll at least rinse off the blade."

Solomon handed the leather scabbard to Watts. "Chomp down on this while we work on the snake bite."

James Watts tilted his head back and closed his eyes.

Thomas held Watts by the arm and cut, making sure not to slit too deeply. His daddy always warned him about folks that got scared and cut so deep around a snake bite that the afflicted person nearly bled to death.

Solomon then leaned down and sucked the blood, spitting the bright red liquid that turned to a brownish hue once it hit the ground. He went back to his horse and found his canteen so he could rinse his mouth.

Thomas cut the tail of his shirt and bandaged the wound after he wiped the first blood away. He stopped and looked down at his hand, the thick red fluid from Watts's body settling between his fingers.

The blood of two brothers on his hands. At least this one was redemptive.

James Watts gazed at him with glistening eyes. "The old preacher up at the prison always said the Lord works in mysterious ways. I guess He does." He wiped his mouth with the back of his hand. "All I've been doing lately is trying to find you to kill you, and here I am now, needin' to thank you for savin' my life."

Thomas patted him on the arm and turned to Solomon. "I guess we need to lift him up on his horse and lead him on back to your house."

Solomon studied his face. "Is that what you want to do?"

Thomas wiped his knife blade on his pants leg. "What else can we do? How far is it to a doctor?"

"It's at least a day's ride. We can't leave him out here."

Solomon kneeled beside Watts. "We need to lift you up on your horse and we'll lead him on in. I know you're in pain, but we have to move you off this damp ground. We'll take you to my place until you're able to ride out."

Watts nodded and closed his eyes.

When Solomon and Thomas lifted him under each of his arms, he winced. They made their way to his horse, his boots scraping the ground beneath him.

"Do you think he'll make it?" Thomas frowned as they placed him in the saddle. Watts's head slumped forward and rested on the saddle horn.

"Only the good Lord knows the answer to that question."

Thomas motioned to Solomon to follow him to the porch. "He's resting good. The snake bite looks better than I ever thought it would. It's been three days and I don't think the skin around the bite is even red anymore."

"It's all according to the amount of venom the snake put into the flesh, you know. Maybe since it had to go through his shirt sleeve, he didn't get as much."

"That may be right." Thomas sighed. "I knew a boy one time in Pineville that nearly lost his hand over a snake bite. I'm glad that James's wound looks good. He may heal all right."

The door to the house opened slightly. "Yes, I think I will, thanks to you two."

Thomas opened the door all the way. "Want to come out here with us?"

"Yes, I'd like to, if it's all right." James hobbled over to a vacant chair. "I don't know what to say to y'all. Here I was, trying to find Thomas to avenge my brother's death, and then the two of y'all saved my life. I know I've been nothin' but trouble, and you could've left me laying out there, and nobody would've ever known. Or you could've finished me off real easy."

Thomas cleared his throat. "But you see, we couldn't do that. The Bible tells us to love our enemies, bless them that curse us, do good to them that hate us. That sums up our situation here, don't you think?"

Thomas peered at James. "I want you to know I am truly sorry for your brother's death. Things were rough down in Beaumont. You probably already heard that. He was drinking heavily that night, and he came at me with a knife. I fought back, but I never intended to kill him."

"I realize that now. Me and my brother have always been a rough lot. Our mama died when we was little, and our daddy ran off and left us with some old people that lived close by. They didn't want us, or maybe they couldn't take care of us. Anyway, we was shifted from place to place until we just ran away when I was fourteen and he was twelve. I always tried to protect him, but he was an angry one. And I was too."

Watts covered his face and sobbed.

Solomon went into the house and returned with a handkerchief. "Here."

Just then they heard one long blow on a horn. Solomon smiled. "That would be Mr. Cain coming to visit."

When he rode into the clearing Solomon went to meet him. "Come on up here and sit awhile."

"Looks like you got company. Mind if an old feller sits with y'all?"

"James, do you feel like having a little company? Mr. Cain would like to sit with us."

James wiped his face with the handkerchief. "No sir, I sure don't mind."

Solomon stepped up to the porch and took his seat again. He leaned against the wall in his ladder-back chair. "We have a lot to tell you, Clark."

Thomas sat and listened for a few minutes, then he let his mind turn to what mattered most—getting back to Pineville to Sarah. He had accomplished what he set out to do, with the Lord's help, of course. He didn't ever remember feeling such satisfaction.

Chapter Twenty-Three

Sarah would speak with Dr. Bailey this afternoon because he asked her to. She had been miserable after she saw Andrew Smith at church. As bad as she hated having to address the situation, it needed to be done. She couldn't avoid this man all the time and nausea rushed through her each time she laid eyes on him.

She wouldn't take the wagon back to town after they'd had lunch and she had turned the children over to Abigail. She would ride Lucky, traveling light and spending as little time as possible discussing any and everything about this man who all of a sudden wanted to be part of her life.

She only waited now because Uncle Marshall insisted on saddling Lucky and bringing him around to her. That was the way her uncle had always been. He wasn't happy unless he was busy helping out in some way. Sometimes she wanted to tell him she could take care of things but it would crush him.

She waited on the back porch and he led Lucky up to meet her. "Sari, I know you're going today because you respect the doc and feel you owe him an explanation. But I think it'll be good for you to clear the air with Andrew."

"I'm sure it will be. I don't know why everyone thinks I should be happy because this man shows up here, saying he's my father. Don't they understand that I've not seen him since I was two years old. Where has he been all this time?"

"I don't know. I recognize him, Sari. I remember him, but I don't know where he's been or what he's done since your mama died. I'm glad you're going today, though. But only because I think it's good for you."

She climbed on Lucky's back and took the reins in her hand. "I won't be gone long."

While she rode to town Sarah tried to think of what she would say, but the ride wasn't quite long enough for that. Before she ever came up with the first thing she would tell him, she was in town and tying Lucky in front of Dr. Bailey's office.

One thing was for sure. Even though she had come to do so, she really didn't care to talk to Andrew Smith.

Before she ever turned the doorknob, Dr. Bailey opened it. "Come in, Sarah."

She twisted her gloves in her hand. "Are we alone?"

"Yes. No one is here but me. I wouldn't have it any other way."

Dr. Bailey walked to his private office with Sarah following. They took their seats. "Andrew is an old friend. He is a dear friend. But I value my relationship with you even more. I've asked you here to see if you will let him speak with you just one time. He said he will leave town after he gets a chance to talk. He feels you deserve some answers from him."

"I may deserve answers, but I can't say he deserves forgiveness."

"I'll let you be the judge of that. Will you consent to talk with him?"

"Yes, I will. But then he has to leave town. Please tell him that."

"He's at the hotel now, waiting for your answer. I'd like to get him and bring him over so we can address this. What do you say?"

Sarah swallowed hard. "Yes, please bring him over. Let's get this done, so he can move on."

Dr. Bailey nodded and left the room. She wiped her sweaty hands on her skirt.

The man must have been waiting by the hotel door and ran

down to the office when Dr. Bailey gave him the signal. Before she even had time to think of what was about to take place, the door opened and shut.

Dr. Bailey ushered him into the room. "Andrew, you may sit in my chair behind the desk. I'll be out here in the reception area if I'm needed."

The door closed behind Dr. Bailey, and she turned to face Andrew Smith. Her heart pounded.

He handed her the basket she had left in the cemetery the day they met. "I wanted to make sure your grandmother's basket made its way back to you."

How did he know the details about the basket?

She thought he would never stop chewing on his lip. Finally, he smiled and said, "Thank you for meeting with me. It's something you probably don't want to do."

Sarah nodded.

"I'd like to explain where I've been for nearly twenty-three years of your life." He cleared his throat and his eyes watered. "I never felt worse than I did the day your mother died. The two of you were everything to me."

She raised her chin. "That's what I was told by everyone who knew you. And that's what I believed before you showed up here."

"You'll never know how sorry I am. When I couldn't save her, I felt a failure I'd never known before. Here I was, a young doctor with such high ideals." Tears flowed from his eyes and ran down his cheeks. He pulled a handkerchief from his vest pocket and wiped his face. "I let your grandfather take you, because I didn't think they would ever forgive me for letting your mother, their only daughter, succumb to influenza. I survived and she didn't. How I wish it could have been the other way around."

He closed his eyes for a moment. "I didn't think I was worthy of your love. I felt responsible for your mother's death and I knew how much she loved you and wanted to raise you."

Andrew opened his eyes. "Of course, I really wasn't responsible for her death. I tried everything to save her, but it didn't happen. Her fever was so high. No matter what I did, it wouldn't go down. I never left her side, and even after all my education and training, my beautiful Katherine died in my arms." He took a deep breath.

"After she died, I thought if your grandparents could care for you until I could get over the shame and remorse, I could come and get you. But I needed time. So, I sent word that I had died."

A lump grew in Sarah's throat. She nodded.

"And I had died. A part of me died with Katherine." Andrew stopped and tugged at his necktie. "Then I began using morphine. Just a little at first. But then more and more. I couldn't make it through a day without it. My life was a mess. You wouldn't have wanted to know me then, I promise."

An odd ache rose in her throat. She looked at her hands.

"But I had a friend, another doctor, who helped me pull myself back up. He helped me shake the morphine habit and convinced me to go to your grandparents and tell them the truth. He said I should raise you as your mother would have wanted."

Andrew gazed into the distance. "Then one day I came to Pineville. I wanted to see you, and I had hopes of taking you with me. I remembered where your grandparents lived, but before I ever made it out there, I saw you and your grandmother coming into town in a little carriage. You were six years old and just as pretty as a picture."

Andrew smiled, but his eyes still brimmed with tears. "The two of you looked so happy. You had on a beautiful dress, and you were smiling and talking with your grandmother. I stepped to the side of the building and hid so she wouldn't see me. I left town and never came back until now."

Through a voice choked with tears, Sarah said, "No more. I don't want to hear any more."

She jumped from the chair and bolted to the front door. Dr. Bailey grabbed her by the arm. "I can't let you leave this way."

"I have to get out of here. I want to be alone. I…I have to be alone."

She ran to Lucky and pulled herself up on the saddle. Tears blurred her eyes, but Lucky sensed where she wanted to go. Before long, she guided her horse down the creek bank, across town where the creek flowed wider than it did near her home.

She wiped her eyes and sat directly on the smooth, white sandbar. Through her father's eyes she had just witnessed her mother's death. He said he didn't interrupt her life because he wanted her to be happy. Her heart ached for him but at the same time his weakness made her stomach turn.

She sat where she first landed when she arrived and let the words her father spoke run through her mind again and again. The creek flowed by her, and she marveled at the way the pine trees stood firm on the other side of the creek. The leaves on the oaks and sweetgums near the bank fluttered from time to time when the wind moved their leaves, but the pines branches never stirred.

Her grandparents had raised her to be like the tall pines— standing firm even when the wind blew. Her father was more like the leaves on the other trees, fluttering when the winds of life came along.

A cool breeze whispered to her in the leaves of the trees behind her and the sun sank lower in the sky. Lucky grazed on the grass sprouting on the creek bank and didn't want to raise his head when Sarah took the reins. She guided him up to the road with a heaviness in her arms and legs.

She trudged along with her head down, knowing it was time to start for home but dreading to go anywhere. When she saw someone standing beside a wagon the road, Sarah gasped.

"Sari, get in the wagon. I'll tie Lucky to the back."

"Uncle Marshall, how long have you been here?"

"I came after the doc showed up at the house and told me you'd left there pretty upset."

She clung to him. "I needed to think. To go over all he said today."

"We thought you would." Uncle Marshall helped her into the wagon.

"Abigail said to come in the back way, up the back staircase and go straight to your room if you'd like. She's with the children and will warm their supper from what she fixed at noon and put them to bed when we finish playing."

Sarah lifted her chin and pushed her shoulders back. "That sounds awfully inviting, but I want to be with my family. I've had plenty of solitude for one afternoon. Besides, I'd like to know if Melissa and John talked you into taking them fishing at the creek by the house. Melissa was planning a fishing trip as soon as she woke up this morning, you know."

"Well, I did take them for a few minutes until Abigail said they needed a nap."

She leaned back against the wagon seat and let out a long sigh. Tonight was the time to live in the present. Acknowledging the past was too much work.

Chapter Twenty-Four

Sarah stared into the darkness. Should she allow herself and her family to have a relationship with her father? Or should she let him walk out of her life one last time?

Why would she not forgive him? How could she feel that she was forgiven by her Lord, and then not pardon someone who had made poor choices or plainly failed to act? This was her family, after all. Her mother was gone, but her father was here, and if she turned him away, she may never get the chance to know him again.

She bolted upright in bed. Why would she deprive her children of knowing their grandfather? She had such joy in the relationship with her own grandparents, what right did she have to turn theirs away?

Yes, she'd light the lamp in her room, dress and find Andrew Smith this morning.

Before long Sarah was dressed in a white shirtwaist and a gray skirt. She joined her Uncle Marshall and Abigail in the kitchen.

"Abigail, I need to get into town this morning and I want to leave before Eliza arrives. Could you stay with the children until she get here?'

"Of course. I don't have anywhere to be today.

Uncle Marshall laid his fork beside his plate. "The sun hasn't come up yet. Where are you headed?"

"I'm going to town to see Andrew before he gets away. The deal was if I met with him and let him explain a few things, he would leave. We met yesterday, but I've decided I'm not quite ready for him to go. I'd like to get to know him a little better."

"That's mighty fine of you, Sari."

"I'm not making any promises about anything, but I have a few more questions. I want to stop him before the first train leaves. I have no idea which direction he's going."

Abigail pulled a chair from the table. "Have some breakfast and sit down a minute."

"Thank you so much, but I really have to do this. I can get something at the hotel."

Uncle Marshall stood and grabbed his hat. "Let me go and see if Earl is out there already."

"I'll do that. You finish your breakfast."

"No, Sari. That's my place."

Sarah sat, shaking her head. "All right. I'll let you. But then I want you to finish your breakfast."

Abigail and Sarah exchanged knowing glances when Uncle Marshall headed out the door. "You can't change him now."

"I know. That's why I let him go."

"I think you're wise to get to know Andrew better. It may take some time, but you'll be glad you did."

"I suppose so. There's so much that none of us realized. I'd also like to understand why he decided to come forward now."

Uncle Marshall appeared in the kitchen and returned to the table. "He'll be up directly."

"Thank you so much. I'll leave as soon as he brings up the wagon." As she watched out the window, little glimmers of light filtered through the pines as the sun made its appearance.

"Here's Mr. Earl now. I'll let you know later how it goes this morning."

"I believe it will go just fine." Uncle Marshall waved.

She had to make it before the first train departed for the day. Or what if he had arranged to have someone take him to a nearby town? After all, she had no idea where he even lived.

She was surprised to see all the activity in town this early. Mr. Wright turned the "Open" sign around at the mercantile, and Mr. Spencer was arriving at the bank.

She stopped in front of the hotel, jumped down to the ground, and opened the lobby door. The first thing she saw was Andrew Smith coming down the stairs with his suitcase in hand. He stopped on the step where he was and smiled at her.

"Good morning. Are you leaving so early?"

He descended the stairs. "A deal is a deal, right?"

"Yes, unless one party requests a change." Sarah glanced to see if the dining room had opened. "Could you have breakfast with me and talk for a few minutes? I realize I know very little about you."

Andrew set his suitcase on the floor. "Of course. Let me see if they'll hold this at the desk."

She went in the dining room and requested a table. As soon as she was seated, he joined her.

"So, do you drink coffee, Andrew?" She noticed that his smile faded when she called him by his first name.

"Yes, I like coffee very much. How about you?"

"I do, too. I'm not being disrespectful by calling you Andrew. It is less formal than Mr. Smith." Sarah peered down at her hands in her lap. "I don't know you well enough to refer to you as my father yet."

"I understand. Believe me when I say I'm just thankful to be sitting with you right now. I was foolish to wait this long. I was a coward."

She studied his face for a moment. Their eye color was identical. "Well, the first thing we have to establish here is that we're moving forward. We can't make up for lost time. So, I need you to refrain from saying things like that. I'm not going to look at you as a coward or a foolish person. I have to believe you did what you thought was the best for me."

"You're so much like Katherine. Positive and caring."

"Now that's the kind of thing I want to hear. I want to know about my mother. What you loved most about her. And where in the world you've been living all this time." She closed her eyes for a few seconds then opened them. "I'd also really like to know why you decided to come forward now."

Mrs. Hill came to take their order. "Sorry it took so long to get here. I'm the only one that's working this morning. Hopefully the lady that works for me will arrive soon. What can I get for you Mrs. Andersson? Mr. Smith eats my homemade biscuits every morning with his eggs."

"Oh he does? I'll take the same."

Mrs. Hill started to walk away then she turned back. "Coffee with one spoon of sugar, Mr. Smith?"

"Yes. Thank you, Mrs. Hill."

Sarah waited until Mrs. Hill left to speak again. "That's how I take mine. Looks like they've learned your habits while you've been here."

"Yes, but I've been here at the hotel for two weeks, so they've certainly learned my likes and dislikes. I didn't want to impose on the Bailey's, and I didn't want to interfere with your friendship with them, so I moved over here after I stayed with them about one week. It's hard to believe I've already been in Pineville for three weeks."

"I don't want to ask you to do something that's not right for you, but can you stay here a little while longer and let us get to know you?"

His eyes sparkled, and his slight smile turned into a wide grin. "Yes, I can stay. Getting to know you and the children is the most important thing for me. I'm so pleased that you asked."

Was this really happening? A shiver moved all the way down her spine. Her father was alive after all.

"I need to make a request. I can't allow you to get to know the children until I have spent some time with you and feel comfortable about that. They are so precious to me."

"I understand. Benjamin told me the kind of mother you are, so I expected as much." Andrew wiped his hand across his forehead. "I will agree with everything you have to say about this situation. I've prayed for so long that I would have the courage to approach you and that you would accept me as your father."

Mrs. Hill brought the coffee. "Do you use sugar, Mrs. Andersson?"

Sarah nodded and touched Andrew's hand. "Why, yes. I do use sugar. One spoon, just like him."

There was so much to learn. But this was a first step. How many more would there be? Only time would tell.

Chapter Twenty-Five

Thomas had a wide grin this morning. He was finally headed back to Pineville. Back to Sarah, Melissa and John. And he felt great satisfaction in the manner that his expected altercation with James Watts had turned out. Now he wanted to get back home and convince Sarah it was time to get married.

Watts was quieter than usual this morning. He sat in a chair at the kitchen table, staring into his coffee cup. Thomas intended to talk to him before he left and admonish him to stay on a good path. He had served his time in prison and paid his debt to society, so now it was up to him.

Solomon came in the house after completing his chores. "I've got Blaze all ready to go. I gave him a good brushing and saddled him for you. My question is, where is that Clementine going to ride?"

"I'm not exactly sure, but I'm thinking she'll ride in front of me. I'll have to see how that works out."

Watts hobbled to the chair with the aid of a crutch. "I need to tell you something before you go."

Thomas sat beside him. "What's that?"

"When I went to Pineville looking for you, I went to your lady's house."

Thomas's body tensed. "You did what?"

"I told the woman at the hotel you were an old friend and asked her where I might find you. She said over at Sarah's house since it was Sunday. And she told me how to get there."

He clenched his fist. "You'd better tell me what happened. And make it fast."

Solomon stood between them. "James, if I were you, I'd start talking."

James's voice shook. "Well, I knocked on the door, and nobody opened it, so I pushed it in. There was a man there, but the lady, Sarah, said she'd handle it and pointed a gun at me the whole time."

"Was there an older man with her?"

"No, he was young. About your age, with light hair."

Thomas's shouted, "What happened? Tell me everything."

"Well, nothing really happened. I thought she was goin' to shoot me, but I don't think she really wanted to. Anyway, the thing that made her the maddest was when a little girl came down the stairs and saw what was going on. But then another lady ran and got her." James's chin trembled. "I didn't hurt nobody. I just wanted to find you. She's the one that told me you were out here in the thicket."

Thomas crossed his arms and glared at James. "Why didn't you tell me this before now? That first day, after we brought you home, I asked you how you knew I was here, and you said the sheriff told you."

"We were all gettin' along and, well, you and Solomon were so nice to me. I thought you'd kick me out. Or worse." James covered his face with his hands.

"I hope you're telling me the truth now."

"Yes, I am. I only told you, because I know you're headed home, and she'll tell you all about it when you get there. But she pointed that old revolver at me the whole time, so I got out of there when I found out what I needed to know."

Thomas chuckled. "Yeah, I know all about that Colt pocket revolver. It was her grandfather's. Believe me, she knows how to use it. Keeps it in her desk."

Solomon slapped Thomas on the back. "Better watch your step."

Thomas grinned. "Okay, boys. I need to hit the trail. If I leave now, I'll be there tomorrow afternoon."

"You camping on the Neches tonight?" Solomon looked down at the floor.

"Yep, that's my plan. Then we'll head in at sun up." Thomas and Solomon shook hands. "I want you to know I appreciate how you helped me. Now, I have a favor to ask of you."

"What would that be?"

"I need you to stand up with me at the wedding."

"Are you sure you want an old backwoodsman like me?'

"Yes, I do. And I won't let you out of it. But we may have to trim that beard a little."

Solomon stroked his beard. "See, that's all women are good for."

Thomas shook his friend's hand. "I'm afraid you're wrong about that."

When Thomas crossed the threshold, James hobbled over to the door. "I might come to Pineville and look you up one day. Got any jobs at that sawmill?"

"I just may, James, if you stay clean."

Thomas shook James Watts's hand. Then he made his way outside to find Blaze.

Solomon followed him out. "I know you came under bad circumstances, but I've enjoyed you being here."

"I couldn't have pulled it off without you." Thomas patted his friend on the arm and grabbed Clementine. "I'll send you word about the wedding."

Thomas situated himself in the saddle, and Clementine settled herself against the pommel. He waved and rode away, heading for Pineville and all he had waiting for him there.

Chapter Twenty-Six

Sarah stared at the invoices Mr. Morgan had placed on her desk. Thomas had been gone two months now, and she had managed to process the orders and approve billing during that time. And she could continue if need be. Fortunately, the procedures Thomas had put in place worked well, and she always had Clyde Morgan, the bookkeeper, to assist in the daily operations in the office.

She could keep the business running in Thomas's absence, but she wasn't so sure about her personal life. She had been busy with the extra duties at the sawmill and the discovery of Andrew Smith when he appeared unannounced, but she couldn't wait until she had Thomas back again. How many sleepless nights had she endured over the last two months, worrying about Thomas and that evil James Watts?

She had so much to tell him. There was no one besides Thomas who could soothe her doubts and fears. Of course, she had her Uncle Marshall and his sweet Abigail to rely on, but Thomas had such insight into her soul. And that was just exactly how she should feel about the man she wanted to spend the rest of her life with.

Even though she ached to hear his voice and feel his hand in hers, she had to be patient. If he didn't accomplish what he set out to do, it could affect him the rest of his life. So, she would wait, and pray for his safety as she had been doing.

Sarah pulled the letter opener from the drawer and opened the envelopes to see what should be handled first. Before she even opened all the mail, the piercing sound of the mill whistle signaled it was noon. Where had the morning gone? She had stopped to visit with Andrew first thing this morning, finding that she learned a little more about him each day, even though she still questioned his absence all these years and his motives for contacting her now. Then she had stopped in at the mercantile so she wouldn't have to do it when she started home.

Someone knocked. She had no time for interruptions today, so she didn't get up from her chair. "Come in, please." Expecting to see Mr. Morgan, she never looked up.

"Is it wise to allow just anyone in your office?"

Sarah's hands quivered. She dropped the letter opener. Almost afraid to look up, she hesitated. What if she only thought it was Thomas's voice?

She heard the unmistakable sound of his footsteps moving toward her, so she raised her head. Sarah felt her lips move into the largest smile she remembered having in a long time.

"Sarah, I can't tell you how much I've missed you." Thomas lifted her in his arms and touched her face with his fingertips.

"Oh, Thomas, finally you're home."

They shared a kiss that was unlike any they'd experienced before. Warmth spread through her entire body.

She stood back and gazed at Thomas. "Oh, my, I've never seen you when you aren't clean shaven."

He rubbed his chin. "I was anxious to get on the trail this morning. And I didn't stop at my place before I came here. But I did stop at your house, and I got to see Melissa and John."

The baying of a hound filled the air. "Is that a dog in our office?"

Clyde Morgan moved through the door holding the puppy. "I couldn't keep her quiet, Thomas. She heard your voice in here."

"Is this your dog, Thomas?"

He reached out to get the pup from Mr. Morgan. "Yes, I'd like for you all to meet Clementine. We rescued her in the woods after her mother was killed."

"She's precious. Did you let the children see her?"

"Yes, they were thrilled with her, and Gus liked her, too."

The door opened again, and Uncle Marshall wandered into the room. "Well, I heard voices, but I didn't know you were here, Thomas." He reached for Thomas's hand. "And look at that hound."

"Meet Clementine."

"Fine looking pup. We'll have her on the trail, won't we Tom?"

"Yes, we will. She has quite a nose on her. I discovered that on the ride home."

"Well, I'm goin' on out and let y'all visit. I'm sure I'll see you later."

"Yes, I'll be around."

Clyde Morgan stepped to the door again. "I need to get back to work. Sorry I couldn't keep the dog quiet."

Thomas nodded and laughed. "That's all right. She has a mind of her own."

Sarah petted Clementine on the neck. "She's so cute. And I love her name." Her smile faded. "I see you're here, safe and sound, but how did things work out? Did you take care of Mr. Watts?"

"Yes. I did take care of him, but not in the way you may be thinking. Me and Solomon found him injured in the woods, so we helped him out, then took care of him at Solomon's place."

Sarah sighed. "What a wonderful resolution. Will he be all right?"

"Yes, he was doing well when I left. He told me that he went to your house and you held a pistol on him. Did everything come out all right?" Thomas rubbed the back of his neck. "I guess I'm wanting to know the truth about what happened that day."

"He forced my front door open, Thomas. He was loud and

boisterous. I had no choice but to protect my home and my family."

Thomas pulled her close to him. "I'm just sorry you had to experience that."

Sarah wrinkled her nose. "I hope I never have to see that man again."

"And you shouldn't. I don't look to hear from him again. But I am satisfied how things ended."

"We have so much to talk about, Thomas. I want to know all the details of the last two months. And I have a lot to tell you, too"

"I know we have a lot to talk about, but I'd like to get to my place and get cleaned up and shave. Why don't I do that and meet you at your house?" Thomas grinned. "Eliza and Abigail told me they were cooking up something special tonight, since I made it home."

"Let me guess. Chicken and dumplings?"

"I don't know. They didn't say." He kissed her lightly on the cheek. "I may have to bring Clementine. She's not used to being left alone."

"Sure. The more the merrier. Hopefully we can be alone after supper to talk, though."

Thomas stacked the envelopes and invoices on the desk. "Leave this for me tomorrow. I'll be here bright and early."

Sarah winked. "I think I will, Thomas. After all, I have a suitor coming to call tonight."

Sarah watched out the window to see if Thomas had arrived yet. She felt like she floated on air this evening. Somehow everything was so right in the world now that Thomas had made it back home. To her, the sun shined brighter all afternoon, the sky was so blue, with not a cloud to be found. Why even the pines were greener than before.

She finally returned to the kitchen to see if Abigail needed help. Uncle Marshall had taken Melissa and John outside with him, since they waited patiently for him to return from work every afternoon. They really didn't mind if they joined him to gather tomatoes from the garden or just sat with him on the porch.

"Abigail, I'm sorry. I haven't been much help, have I? I've been so anxious for Thomas to arrive."

"You've been plenty of help. The dining room table looks beautiful."

She sighed. "I enjoy using my grandmother's table cloths and napkins so much. Besides being beautiful, they bring back such happy memories. And I was able to pick enough flowers to fill a vase."

Abigail removed her apron and sat down at the kitchen table. "Everything's ready now. We just need Thomas and Charles to get here. I'm sure Marshall and the children will be in soon."

When someone knocked on the front door, she scurried to throw it open.

"Charles. It's you. Come in."

"Are you sure, Sarah?" He chuckled. "You seem pretty disappointed to see me."

"Oh, come in. I thought you were Thomas. I'm sorry."

Charles stepped inside, then Sarah pushed past him. "Oh, I see him. He and Blaze are coming around the curve. Go on in. Your mother is in the kitchen."

Sarah slammed the door behind her and waited at the gate for Thomas. When he came closer, she noticed Clementine riding with him. "What ever will you do when she gets too big for the saddle?"

"I don't know. I've been wondering about that. I suppose she'll have to follow me on foot."

He met her at the gate and leaned in to kiss her. "It's so good to see you. I can't believe I'm finally home."

She ran her fingers across his freshly shaven skin. "You had me a little worried this afternoon. I was afraid you had taken on the ways of a backwoodsman."

"No worries there. I enjoyed my time with Solomon, but I'm happy to be back home."

"Come on in. Supper's ready. Abigail and Eliza cooked everything you like. We're having chicken and dumplings, butter beans, fresh tomatoes and cornbread."

"I'm starving. Today I was in such a hurry to get here and see you and the children that I never ate anything after breakfast."

She took his hand in hers, and they strolled to the porch, with Clementine following, of course.

Sarah smoothed her skirt before she sat beside Thomas in the parlor. "You did a wonderful job telling the children a story. I'm almost certain you added a few things to make it more exciting."

Thomas lowered himself onto the settee. "Did you like the part about the lion in the pasture? I thought it sounded better than a plain old bobcat."

"Yes, until they learn there are no lions in East Texas."

Thomas rubbed his belly. "I think I ate a little too much tonight. I'd grown a little tired of venison and squirrel. Between Abigail and Eliza, that was quite a spread."

"So, your friend Solomon likes wild game?"

"I guess so. He also cooked up some pretty good catfish a few times. He fishes and hunts when he pleases, so he just goes out and gets whatever he wants. But he's not fond of chicken. He has a few laying hens, but that's all."

"You left Solomon to deal with James Watts? He must be a good friend."

"He is. Watts is still not able to ride out, and Solomon knew how anxious I was to get home. Like I said earlier, we found Watts in a really bad predicament. He couldn't even move. At that point he called for help on his horn, and we followed the sound, never dreaming it was him."

"It couldn't have worked out better for either of you. I'm so glad that's behind you. Now you can finally move forward. And I suppose Mr. Watts can, too."

Thomas rose from the settee and kneeled on one knee. His pulse raced. "I'd like for us to move forward together, Sarah. You, me, Melissa and John."

Sarah gasped softly.

"Will you marry me, Sarah?"

Sarah's eyes filled with tears. "Yes. You know I will."

They both stood and met in an embrace. He whispered in her ear. "I don't want to wait anymore. I want to marry as soon as we can. This has been too long in coming."

Sarah stood back and stared at Thomas. "What do you mean? I thought we agreed to wait until August. You know, when Nils has been gone for a year." She turned her back to him. "I thought it would be more respectful."

"I'll wait if you insist. But I'm ready for us to be a family."

She faced him. "I'm ready, too. But I want to do the right thing. I just thought the whole time that's what we'd do. So, I need to give it some thought. Of course, I want to be Mrs. Thomas Carson. With all my heart." She giggled. "And a June wedding would be so lovely."

Thomas pushed her hair back from her face. "You think it over and let me know. I'm ready whenever you are."

She needed some time to think, that was all. Or was it?

Chapter Twenty-Seven

Sarah stepped into the kitchen just as Uncle Marshall pushed wood into the stove. "Sari, what are you doing up so early? Now that I think about it, you've been up early a lot of times lately. My habits are rubbing off on you."

"I have some news. Some wonderful news. Thomas and I are getting married."

Uncle Marshall dropped the remaining piece of wood he held. At the thud, she jumped. He ran to her side. "I'm so happy. You and Thomas can have a great life together. Let's go wake Abigail up and tell her."

"No, not yet. I want to ask you something first. Will you do the honor of walking in with me at the ceremony?"

Uncle Marshall's eyes glistened with tears. "You know I will. I'll be proud to do that for sure."

"I couldn't sleep last night after Thomas and I talked. He wants to get married right away, but I told him I wanted to wait until August, you know, until Nils has been gone a year. It is the respectful thing to do. But then I began to ponder the happiness we can begin sharing now. So, I'm going to tell Thomas today that I would like to set our wedding date on June twenty-second. What do you think?"

"Well, that sounds just right. That's a little over one month away. You know, I understand you wanted to wait a year's time, but you also need to start building a life with you and Thomas and those young'uns."

"Let's go wake Abigail. She'll want to help me make plans."

"Plans for what? I heard a crashing sound and Marshall talking in here, so I came to see if something's wrong." Abigail tied the belt of her wrapper around her as she walked.

"Sit down, Abigail. While Uncle Marshall gets the stove going and the water boiling for the coffee, I'll tell you." Sarah pulled a chair away from the round oak table and motioned for Abigail to sit there.

Sarah took the chair across from her. "Thomas and I are getting married. We talked last night. I know I had planned to wait until August or after, but I think now it will be June twenty-second."

Abigail jumped up and came around to hug Sarah. "So those are the plans we're talking about. I'm so happy for you and Thomas. I think you're wise to go ahead and begin this new life. The children absolutely love Thomas."

"Yes, they'll be delighted. So, since I've told the two of you, and I'll head straight to the sawmill this morning to tell Thomas I'd like to make June twenty-second the official date, then we can tell everyone in town."

Uncle Marshall trudged over to the table. "What about Andrew? Don't you want him to walk you into the ceremony? He is your father."

"I've already considered that. I'll invite him to the wedding, but he really can't expect weeks of knowing him to equate with the time you've cared for me and I for you. He'll have to understand."

"Whatever you say. I don't want to get in the way of anything you need to do with him."

She touched Uncle Marshall's hand. "I appreciate that. But remember, this is a happy time for our family. We're going to have great fun planning our wedding."

The clock chimed. "I'll go on up and get dressed so I can tell Eliza the news, then head to the sawmill to see Thomas."

She peeked at her sleeping children. Her decision was the

correct one. No one could ever really take the place of their father, but Thomas Carson would do his best. That was a fact.

She couldn't tell Marshall and Abigail without letting Eliza in on the news. And she had known Eliza would be excited. Sarah could always count on her housekeeper who was indeed a wonderful friend, to share news with, whether it was good or bad.

Thomas was sure to have a busy time on his first day back, but Sarah wanted to see him first thing and let him know she had decided on a June wedding. As soon as she left home, she began thinking of how she would surprise him with the news. Should she write a letter and leave it on his desk and then hide in the hall? Or maybe she should just tell him.

Sarah whistled a tune nearly all the way to the sawmill. Ecstatic at the thought of the wedding, she was even more happy that she and Thomas would be sharing their life together.

She let herself in his office and sat in the chair behind his desk. He would be in to start his work after he made his rounds out in the mill. That may take a little extra time today, since it was his first day back.

Sarah pulled a piece of paper and a pencil from the desk drawer. She titled the list, "Wedding for Sarah and Thomas."

She added the date, but not the time yet. She needed to consult him about that. Since it would be in June, she thought they should probably set it to begin just before the sun would go down, when it was cooler.

She had to smile when she wrote the words flower girl and ring bearer. She knew two beautiful children who could fit perfectly in those roles.

Of course, she would ask Lucy today to be her maid of honor and she knew Thomas had already asked Solomon to be his best man.

Just then the door opened, and Thomas stood for a moment and gazed at her. "What a surprise. I didn't expect to see you here."

"I wanted to talk to you this morning and tell you something I decided."

Thomas moved over and sat on the edge of the desk. "What would that be?"

Sarah stared directly in his eyes. "I would like to become Mrs. Thomas Carson on June twenty-second."

He pulled her up to face him. "That's wonderful news. But, are you sure?"

"Yes. I'm sure. I've begun to make wedding plans. So, I suspect you'd better let your best man know. You said it may take a little time to contact him."

"Yes, it will. I can't wait for him to meet you. I hope he can come and be here with me a little while before the wedding."

Thomas glanced up to the ceiling. "I know I've been absent awhile from the mill, but that gives me nearly one month to get everything caught up here before the wedding. I'd like for us to go on a short trip after the ceremony. Just the two of us."

"Yes, I think we should do that. We definitely need some time alone. And I'll have Uncle Marshall and Abigail to stay with the children. That's a perfect way to begin our new life together."

"Sarah, we haven't talked about a ring. I'd like for you to tell me what you want to wear."

"Well, I already have the ring, so you don't have to worry about that. It's my grandmother's ring. My grandfather gave it to her on their wedding day many years ago."

She tilted her head a little. "Actually, it's one of my most prized possessions. I can't believe I haven't mentioned it."

"I...I don't really want to ask this question, but I have to. Did you use this ring when you married before?"

Sarah shook her head. "No, Thomas. I'm sorry, I should have

explained. My grandmother was still living when Nils and I married, and she wore it every day. She gave it to me before she died." She placed her hand over her heart. "It's such a sentimental item for me. I tucked it away in a jewelry box at home that belonged to her. I'll show it to you and you'll see it's simple, but special, you know. Their initials are engraved inside, along with the date of their marriage. I thought we could add our initials and wedding date later."

Thomas nodded. "That ring was the symbol of a very happy union. I trust our marriage will be a happy one, too."

"Yes, I know it will be. I love you so much."

Thomas took her in his arms. "And I love you."

After a few moments she moved from his embrace. "I'm happy with our decision to marry in June."

"I'm pleased, too. But I don't want you to feel pressured. It's ultimately your decision."

"Yes, I understand. I'm happy with our plans."

Sarah smiled and grabbed her handbag. "I know you have lots to do today and I'm not going to get in your way. Can we expect you for supper tonight?"

"Sure. We need to tell the children about our wedding plans, if you haven't already. I love Melissa and John, and I want to be there for them."

"Yes, I know. And we're going to have a wonderful family." She smoothed his hair into place. "And speaking of family, I'm going now to tell Andrew about our plans. I don't want him to hear it from other people first."

"I don't know what to think of this fella. I'm anxious to meet him and see what he's like." Thomas rubbed the back of his neck. "But I still can't get used to the fact that he hasn't been around."

"I know. Like I said, I've decided to get acquainted with him and see if I can understand it all."

She made her way to the door. "We'll see you this evening. I won't mention a word to the children until we're all together."

Once she was outside and in the wagon, she guided the horses directly to the hotel. When she pushed open the door, she came face to face with Andrew. "Good morning. I hoped I would find you here."

"Sarah, good morning. Let's go back in. Perhaps you'd like a cup of coffee?"

"That would be nice. I hoped we could visit for a few minutes."

They walked in the hotel and into the dining room. As soon as they were seated, Mrs. Hill came over to take their order. "What can I get for you today?"

"We'd both like coffee, I know. I just finished breakfast not too long ago, so I don't care for anything else. Sarah, would you like something?"

"No, just coffee for me."

Once Mrs. Hill had moved away, Sarah leaned in closer to Andrew. "I have some news to share with you. Thomas Carson and I plan to marry in June."

Andrews's eyes filled with tears. "I'm so happy for you. And I'm anxious to meet him. I know you told me he manages the Adams Sawmill for you."

"Yes, he does. But we were friends all our lives. And our relationship has grown with time."

Mrs. Hill set their cups of coffee on the table. They resumed their conversation when she walked away. "Congratulations, Sarah. If there's anything I can do to help, please let me know."

"We'd be honored for you to attend. The date is June twenty-second."

"And I'll be honored to be in attendance." With his napkin, Andrew wiped a tear that escaped from his eye, then he cleared his throat. "Looks like I may be in Pineville for a while so I'm headed over to the county seat this morning to file my certificate with the District Clerk's office."

"Certificate?"

"When you practice medicine in Texas, you furnish your diploma to the State Board of Medical Examiners, and they issue a certificate, verifying you meet the required standards. Then it has to be filed in the county where you practice. Benjamin and I talked yesterday about me helping him out at the office. He planned to discuss it with you since he's here as part of the Adams Sawmill."

"Every sawmill town, large or small, does require a doctor. We have to be prepared for the injuries that come along with this industry and the families of the workers have medical needs, too. I don't have a problem with you doing that. I see it as a bonus for us." Sarah pressed her lips together for a moment. "We only have a budget for one full-time physician, but we could hire you on a part-time basis. I know Dr. Bailey has more than he can handle some days. And I feel like he rarely takes time off, because he knows there's no one else to cover for him."

"I don't require payment for my services. I've worked for years and never had much to spend my money on. I do want to keep practicing medicine though, so if you'll allow me, I'll help Benjamin out when he needs me."

"That's wonderful. When I leave here, I'll stop by and talk with him. But I insist you accept a house furnished by the mill. We have a couple of vacant ones. The mill manager's house would be a good one for you. It's nice and roomy and Thomas lives on his family farm, so he doesn't need it. Unless you'd rather stay at the hotel."

"No, I am a little weary of living at the hotel. I'd be happy to move into the house you mentioned."

"Then it's set. I'll have someone go in and give it a good cleaning before you move in. It's been vacant since I purchased the sawmill."

Andrew settled back in his chair. "I'm excited to be a part of this town and to have a chance to know you and your family.

You'll never know how much this means."

No, she didn't know how much it meant. She prayed that as time went on she would understand why he deserted her so long ago.

Chapter Twenty-Eight

Thomas walked to the deck to check the supply of logs in the millpond. When he was satisfied with his findings, he turned to face Clyde Morgan.

"Thomas, there's a man waiting in your office. He says his name is Solomon Brown and he also says he is a friend of yours. I let him wait, but…"

Thomas chuckled. "He is a friend, Clyde. A close one. He's a backwoodsman, but he's a fine human being. Don't let that beard and long hair fool you."

"I'm sorry. I let him wait in your office, but I was a little worried."

Thomas hurried to his office, anxious to see Solomon. He looked inside, ready to greet his friend, but he wasn't there. He checked Sarah's office. Maybe Solomon went in the wrong door, but he wasn't there. Finally, he knocked on Clyde Morgan's office door. "He's not in there. I wonder where he could have gone?"

"I don't know. I told him to wait in there."

Thomas walked outside to try to locate Solomon. There was no sign of him anywhere.

Thomas rubbed his chin, then made his way back to Clyde's office. "I don't see him, so I'm going to ride on down to the mercantile and see if he may have gone there. I won't be gone long."

When had Solomon arrived in Pineville? Had he camped the night before instead of coming out to his place? All along the route

145

to town, he kept an eye out for his friend. There was no sign of him anywhere.

Thomas tied Blaze in front of the mercantile and raced inside.

Walter Wright greeted him. "How can I help you today?"

"I'm trying to find my friend. I thought he may have come in here."

"Does he have long brown hair and a beard?"

Thomas nodded. "Yes, he does. Have you seen him?"

Walter Wright grinned. "The man I described stuck his head in the door and asked where the barbershop is located."

Thomas thanked Mr. Wright and crossed the street to the barbershop. He glanced in the window to see if there was any sign of Solomon. Just then a stranger approached him and extended his hand. "Thomas, I got here as quick as I could."

Thomas's eyes widened. "Solomon, is that you?"

"It's me."

"I didn't recognize you. I haven't seen you without the beard since you were old enough to grow one."

"Yeah. I feel kind of strange right now. But I noticed no one else was so, you know, bushy. Then the man at your office seemed down right disturbed by the way I looked."

Thomas patted Solomon on the back. "I don't want you to feel you needed to change on my account, but you look great." He stood back and took another long look. "You'll have the girls swarming around you."

"I doubt that. Hey, aren't you supposed to be at work?"

"Yes, I am. But I came looking for you. Do you want to go back to the mill with me or ride on out and get settled at my place?"

"I guess I'll have to stay with you until quitting time. I got here last night a little later than I'd planned, and I don't know where you live. There was no one around to ask, so I just camped out in the woods, not too far from the sawmill."

"Come on with me. I'll enjoy having you with me today. And

Marilyn Peveto

I can show you how everything works at the mill."

They crossed the street to get their horses when Thomas spotted Lucy Bailey on the sidewalk by her father's office.

"Lucy, good morning."

She waved, then hurried over to greet him. "Thomas, we're all so thankful you made it home safely."

He removed his hat and smiled. "I'd like you to meet my friend, Solomon Brown. He'll be standing up with me at the wedding."

She extended her hand. "So glad to meet you. I'll be doing the same with Sarah."

Solomon reached out to shake her hand and Thomas noticed his friend's hand trembled.

She looked over her shoulder. "I'd better be going. I'm supposed to help out at my dad's office today, and he always thinks I'm late for some reason." She hurried in the direction of Dr. Bailey's office.

"That's Sarah's best friend. And she's a friend of mine, too. We all grew up here in Pineville." Thomas chuckled. "And her father always thinks she's late to work at his office, because she is."

Solomon sighed. "I think she's the most beautiful woman I've ever seen."

"Oh, you do? Better reserve your judgement until tonight when you meet Sarah."

"I'm anxious to meet your Sarah." Solomon turned and stared in the direction of the mercantile. "Instead of going back to the mill with you right now, I think I'll head on over to Wright's and see about buying some clothes. Over in the thicket I don't require much, but I think I may need a few things so I can be more presentable."

"That's fine, if that's what you want to do. But I'm also fine with the Solomon from the Big Thicket."

"I know you are. And that's one thing I like about you. I'll always be a backwoodsman, but I'm ready to broaden my horizons a bit."

Thomas watched Solomon stride in the direction of the mercantile. His friend's hair was thick and full. His jaw line had a chiseled appearance. And his brown eyes sparkled without the hair on his face obscuring them. New clothes. Clean shaven. A haircut. What should he make of all that?

Chapter Twenty-Nine

Sarah closed her eyes while the porch swing swayed. "Solomon is delightful, Thomas."

"He's having a great time tonight. I figured Marshall would like to be in bed by now, but I still hear them laughing in there."

"They really hit it off, didn't they?" Sarah took a deep breath. "And now, I can't believe we're finally together and planning our wedding."

Thomas pushed her hair away from her face. "I wish June would hurry and get here. I also wish Marshall and Abigail would stay with us. There's plenty of room in this big house."

"I know. I'll talk to them again. They could stay until they get their house built out near the river. If I hadn't urged Andrew to take the mill superintendent's house, they could stay there."

"Sarah, I really need to meet Mr. Smith. I've noticed him in town, but we've never been introduced."

Her posture straightened. "I usually visit with him in the morning at the dining room at the hotel. Now that he's moving into a house, I'll have to do things differently." Sarah crossed her arms. "I can't invite him here. I want to get to know him better before I introduce him into the children's lives."

"What are you afraid of?"

"I don't know. He's just a stranger to me. I honestly don't know what to think."

"Let's ask him to meet us for lunch tomorrow at the hotel. It's easier for me to get away at noon than the morning. What do you say?"

"I'll check with him first thing in the morning, then I'll let you know when I get to the mill."

Thomas pulled her closer. "Pretty soon we'll have lots of nights like this. And I can hardly wait."

Sarah stopped in front of the hotel and placed her handbag on her arm. Before she ever stepped down from the wagon Andrew came out of the hotel. "Could I see you for a moment?"

He looked in her direction, then smiled. "Certainly."

Once Andrew stood beside the wagon, he extended his hand. "Would you like to come in and visit?"

"Actually, I wanted to see if you could meet at noon in the dining room at the hotel. It's time you met Thomas. He's really anxious to get to know you."

"And I'm anxious to meet him. I'll be here before noon and get a table where we'll have some privacy."

"We'll see you then." Sarah waved when Andrew walked away.

She arrived at the sawmill mid-morning and went directly to her office. Since Thomas was back home, she didn't have as much to do here, but she could make lists for the upcoming wedding. Her life at home was busier and fuller than ever before with the children, Thomas visiting at night, and time spent with Uncle Marshall and Abigail. The fuller life equated to a happier life in her eyes.

But sometimes she couldn't imagine where Andrew figured in all of this. She had no past memories with him. She had no current feelings except those of responsibility. Only time would tell what would transpire.

Thomas and Solomon talked together before they entered

Thomas's office. Even the sound of Thomas's voice brought an instant smile.

After Solomon left to find Uncle Marshall, Thomas knocked at her door. "Come in, please."

"Good morning." Thomas leaned across the desk and brushed his lips across hers. "I've shown Solomon around the mill and he's quite impressed"

"Perhaps we should offer him a job."

"I don't think he's ready to commit to a life here, but he's enjoying his visit so far."

"I meant to ask how he received his letter from you so soon. You told me it would take a while to contact him."

"Usually it does. But this time Mr. and Mrs. Cain had business in Batson, so they took the letter back to him. I had only hoped he would get it in enough time to travel to the wedding since it's nearly a two-day journey by horseback."

"You know, I'd like to go to his place one day. Not any time soon, mind you. But someday."

"I have big plans to take John there to hunt when he's a little older."

"Make that much older." Sarah swatted at Thomas's arm.

"So do we have lunch plans with your father?"

"Yes."

"I've heard he's nice. I'm ready to meet him."

"What about Solomon? Will he stay here all day?"

"No, he's going on back out to the farm. He's the sort of man who likes to stay busy, so he's going to do some work around the place."

"Can you leave now? Andrew said he'd be there a little early."

"Yes, I can. Let me tell Mr. Morgan we're going."

Sarah tucked the list she had been working on into the drawer and strolled to the door. Thomas took her arm in his, and they made their way to her wagon.

She relaxed against Thomas while he steered the horses on the short trip to town. Peering into the pine forest she saw a magnolia tree with a huge blossom.

"Look, Thomas, the magnolias are blooming. I think we'll use some in our wedding. The fragrance is so lovely."

"I'm glad you're tending to all that. I'll go along with whatever you have in mind, within reason, of course."

"That's good to know because I have a lot of plans in mind. Of course we'll ask Brother Maxwell to perform the ceremony. And we'll invite everyone."

"Everyone?"

"Sure. Everyone."

"All right. Then I'll whisk you away for a few days. How does that sound?"

"Absolutely marvelous."

"So, before we get inside to talk to Andrew, I wondered if he is playing a part in our wedding plans?"

Sarah stood so Thomas could help her down from the wagon. "I invited him, that's all. He's welcome to come."

"Who will walk you down the aisle?"

"Uncle Marshall. My sweet, loving, Uncle Marshall."

Just then Andrew entered the hotel. "I see Dr. Smith now. Let's join him."

Andrew waited for them at a table near the back of the dining room. When they approached the table, he stood. "Hello, my dear Sarah. And this must be Thomas. Glad to meet you."

Thomas grabbed Andrew's hand and shook it. Once they were seated, Andrew addressed Thomas. "I've heard so much about you from Sarah."

"And Sarah has told me about you."

Mrs. Hill came to the table to offer the lunch menu items. "Fried chicken or pork, mashed potatoes, and peas. And of course, our biscuits and cornbread." She handed them the menus. "But if you have a hankering for something else, you can always order from the menu. Don't forget, we have pear pie and dewberry cobbler for dessert. Either of those would be delicious with a cup of coffee after your meal."

Once they made their selections, Thomas turned his attention to Andrew. "So, how do you like living in Pineville?"

Andrew turned to Sarah and smiled. "I'm enjoying it very much. I came here for one reason—to try to get to know Sarah and her family. I've admitted to Sarah and anyone else who will listen that I made a cowardly decision to ignore the fact that I had a daughter. I grieved her mother's death so deeply and felt totally inadequate when it came to raising a child." Andrew shrugged. "So inadequate that I lied about my own death."

Sarah sat back and watched the interaction between the two men. She felt completely at ease since Thomas was here with her. Usually during her visits with Andrew, she had a tightness in her neck and a knot in her stomach. It was like she was defensive against his show of affection for her, and at the same time, almost craving his devotion.

Thomas closed his eyes for a moment after Andrew admitted to his abandonment of Sarah. "I can't even begin to imagine how you felt. But then again, I can't imagine how you could let her go." Thomas took Sarah by the hand. "You're very fortunate you've been given the chance to get to know her."

Andrew cleared his throat. "Believe me, I understand. I've regretted this decision from the day I made it. But I also didn't want to upset her life when she was perfectly happy, growing up with her loving grandparents. As the years went by, my longing to be with her became stronger, so I had to take a chance."

Thomas nodded. "I'd say you and Sarah have an opportunity to have some kind of relationship. But, you need to understand she'll have to take it one day at a time."

Andrew's eyes glowed. "I'm so appreciative of the chance my

daughter is giving me. And I'm very content with one day at a time."

Mrs. Hill came to the table with a tray full of food. Sarah didn't feel hungry until the golden fried chicken was placed in front of her. The black-eyed peas, cooked with a little bacon, and the creamy mashed potatoes, made her mouth water.

"So, what will it be, pear pie or dewberry cobbler?"

Simultaneously Sarah and Andrew answered, "Dewberry cobbler." All three of them burst into laughter. Once the laughter ended, Thomas said, "I'll have pear pie."

When Mrs. Hill walked away, Andrew spoke. "For the last few years I've lived in Houston, working at St. Joseph's Hospital." He laid the napkin in his lap. "I'm not fond of the city, but I always felt like I was hiding, or should be. And that's a good place to live if you don't want folks knowing your past."

Andrew gazed at Sarah and Thomas, and his eyes narrowed. "And the direct opposite is Pineville, where everyone demands to know your past. But, I came here to face my past and the awful mistakes I made with you. I'm just sorry it took so long for me to come."

Sarah glanced at him. "Yes, you are facing your past. And your mistakes."

"I'd love to meet your children one day, Sarah."

The tension rose in her neck. Then came the knot in her stomach. "I'm not ready for you to meet them yet. I'll let you know when the time is right."

She pushed her plate back a little. Her appetite had vanished. It really wasn't important if they both liked their coffee with one spoon of sugar and both liked dewberry cobbler. No matter how hard she tried, she didn't know Andrew Smith. And maybe she never would.

Chapter Thirty

Sarah watched for Eliza at the back door. She couldn't wait to discuss the wedding plans she had made, especially the ones that included her.

Her grandmother reminded her often when she was growing up that a watched pot never boils, so she made her way back to the kitchen table. She was ready to get to the mercantile to look at fabric and also to get John a haircut. His blond hair was reaching down into his collar.

The knob turned, and Eliza walked through the door.

"Come sit down for a moment. I need to talk to you before the children and I leave for town."

Eliza grinned and grabbed her apron from the hook on the wall.

Sarah patted the chair beside her. "You sit here, and I'll get you a cup of coffee. I've already had way too much this morning."

Once Sarah was seated again, she pushed the piece of paper titled, "Andersson-Carson wedding" over to Eliza. "I thought that sounded really official. Don't you think so?"

"Yes, it does."

"This is what I've decided. I want you to be in the wedding, but I also know you won't be comfortable with that. But, I don't want you here working and serving on this important day." Sarah touched Eliza on the arm. "You will preside over the gift table at the reception. I'm buying fabric for your dress today, if they have what I like at the mercantile. Your Auntie Corine will sew it just like Lucy's, but in a different color, and you will wear a corsage."

Eliza's eyes filled with tears and she pulled her apron up to wipe the edges of her eyes. "You don't have to do this. I can't expect to be up there with all the other people."

"If you want me to be happy, you have to play a part in our special day as a friend, not an employee. What do you say?"

"I will do it, but who will be looking after all the food?"

"You will hopefully help me find some people to cook and serve. Abigail will oversee that job, and you can help boss them, too."

Eliza chuckled. "I'll do it then. Thank you so much."

Sarah stood with her wedding list in hand. "Now I'll get the children and head to town. Abigail is combing Melissa's hair upstairs. She helped me with them this morning, so we could get an early start. Of course, I didn't tell John he is going for a haircut, because he doesn't like the barbershop."

Eliza stirred her coffee. "A piece of candy from the mercantile will probably be what he needs to soften the news."

"I think you're right. A piece of candy will help." Sarah straightened the collar on her blouse. "Thank you, Eliza, for agreeing to serve with us at the wedding. And I hope you'll bring Frank and Ruthie and Tillie."

"Yes, I'll surely bring my family. My Auntie Corine said you wanted her to be there at the wedding, then if there are any last-minute alterations, she can help out."

"Your auntie is such a wonderful seamstress. I'm honored for her to make the dresses."

Sarah ran from the room and took the wedding list to its place in her desk. She then worked her way up the stairs, two at a time.

When she and the children had settled into the wagon, she was confident they would accomplish all they needed to on this day. An early start made things go better.

The haircut was the first task of the day, and John behaved so much better after he was promised candy at the mercantile if he sat still in the chair. They moved across the street to Wright's Mercantile and Sarah browsed in the material section before she let the children have the hard, sticky candy from the jar on the counter. Since her dress was to be a pale blue, she had her heart set on a light yellow for Lucy. The fabric for her dress was on order, but perhaps she could find some things at the mercantile for others in the wedding so Mrs. Corine could start on the dresses.

Melissa and John squirmed and whined while shopping for fabric, but she felt like she found some things to come back and look at again the next day when the children weren't with her. She lingered over the display of lace, since the selection was impressive for the small-town store. The one that caught her attention the most was the Irish lace. She knew she would want some portion of it on her wedding dress. But once the children began rolling on the floor of the mercantile, it was time to go.

They moved to the front of the store, so she could hold the children up on the counter to choose their candy. This treat was one they never tired of. After they made their selections, Sarah and the children sauntered out to the sidewalk.

A display of hats graced the window of the mercantile. "Melissa and John, sit here on the bench and enjoy your candy while I look."

From the corner of her eye, she caught a glimpse of Andrew standing in front of Dr. Bailey's office, watching her and the children. She felt the heat rise in her face. *I can't tell him not to look at us.*

She almost walked away from the window display, but Melissa and John were enjoying their hard candy. They both licked the pieces and would chomp on them when they became smaller and more manageable in their mouths.

Turning back to the millinery, she would let them finish their treat, then she would put them in the wagon and head back home.

Suddenly John screamed. A cold shiver ran the length of

Sarah's spine. But it was Melissa whose face was red and her eyes bulged. Andrew raced to her daughter's side. He stood her up and raised her arms, then he began compressions on her chest and throat.

Sarah's heart raced, and tears streamed down her face. "Melissa, oh my baby…"

Without warning the hard, red disc shot from Melissa's throat and landed on the wooden sidewalk beneath their feet. Andrew lifted Melissa into his arms and ran to Dr. Bailey's office. Sarah reached down and grabbed John.

She rushed into the doctor's office. "Where is she? Where is my daughter?"

Dr. Bailey called out, "Second room on the left."

Sarah let John down and took him by the hand. They ran to the examining room. Melissa was stretched out on the table with Andrew on one side and Dr. Bailey on the other. Andrew examined her mouth and throat while Dr. Bailey listened to her chest.

Sarah took her place at the end of the table. Melissa obeyed the doctor's commands. How could her daughter be so calm after such a frightening experience?

Andrew pulled Melissa to a sitting position. "Thank heavens your airways are clear. I had seen these external chest compressions used at St. Joseph's. I didn't know my first patient to use them on would be my gr—um, Melissa."

Melissa blinked and shook her head. "How do you know my name?"

Sarah stepped to her side. "Dr. Smith is someone I know, and I told him your name. Isn't that right, Dr. Smith?"

"Yes. That's right. And I'm glad to finally meet you, Melissa. And John, too."

John stood beside Sarah and kept his eyes on his sister.

Sarah stroked Melissa's face. "Is it all right for me to take her home?"

Dr. Bailey glanced at Andrew. "What do you say, Andrew? You're the one who administered emergency treatment and saved her life."

Andrew patted Melissa's head. "I think her mother will watch her closely, so that will be fine. I will carry her to your wagon, though. She needs to take it easy this afternoon. Her throat may be scratchy, and her chest and throat area may be tender after the compressions."

Sarah followed Andrew as he carried her little daughter to the wagon. Dr. Bailey touched Sarah's arm. "I'm so thankful that Andrew saw what happened and stepped in."

Sarah couldn't speak, so she nodded. Andrew whispered to Melissa. "I know you'll feel better in a little while, honey. Get your mother to read you a story and maybe make you some soft pudding." Melissa nodded.

When they arrived at the wagon, Andrew climbed up with Melissa and sat her on the front seat. He let himself down and extended his hand to Sarah. She allowed him to help her up in the wagon. Then he grabbed John and placed him on the seat beside them.

Her hands trembled when she took the leads for the wagon. How could she have been so unsympathetic to her father?

"Andrew, I think the time has come. Could you join us for supper tonight at six?"

"Yes, I'd love to." He turned toward Dr. Bailey's office.

"Andrew, wait."

He faced Sarah. "Yes?"

"I almost forgot to thank you for saving Melissa."

"Oh, no need to thank me. I'm so happy I was there."

So many thoughts ran through her mind and collided that she paused and closed her eyes for a few seconds. One thing was certain. She thanked the good Lord above for sending her father to be by her side today.

Chapter Thirty-One

Thomas waited on the porch until Sarah answered the door. "Do you have a few minutes to stay out here with me?"

"Sure. I always have time for you." She sat in the swing and patted the place beside her.

"I'm so thankful that Melissa is all right." Thomas's mouth went dry at the thought of her choking on the candy earlier in the day. "I appreciate you asking Dr. Bailey to send me word. He said you had to go on home with the children. And you're sure she's feeling good?"

"She seems fine now. In fact, she seems to have forgotten it altogether. It's not that way for me, though. I keep thinking about the helpless feeling I had, until Andrew ran to her side."

"I'm so glad he got to her in time. It's important to him to get to know you and the children, so it's good you invited him for dinner this evening." Thomas stroked her arm. "Of course, I understand your feelings, too."

Sarah sighed and sat back in the swing. "I finally feel more peaceful regarding my relationship with him. He saved Melissa's life, of course, but he was so gentle with her. And loving. The children shouldn't miss out on their grandfather's affection because of my ill feelings toward him."

Thomas nodded. "It's not been easy. But maybe if you concentrate on their relationship and not worry about yours, things will work out."

"I'll have to keep that in mind." Sarah grinned and stared at

Thomas. "I also invited Lucy over tonight, so we're having a little celebration, I suppose."

"Solomon will love that. He thought Lucy was beautiful the day he met her."

"Well, I thought it would help if they got together a few times before the wedding so they could feel comfortable with each other. And, the more people we have around the table at supper will make the conversation easier. I still don't know what to say to Andrew most of the time."

Thomas kissed her on the forehead. "I'll wait out here for Solomon if you'd like to go in and give Abigail a hand."

"Yes, I'd like that. She and Eliza cooked most everything this afternoon, but we still need to set the table in the dining room. Oh, we also invited Charles Griffin."

"Good. That will give us a chance to introduce him to Solomon."

"Come in the house when you grow tired of being outside. But just remember, we may put you to work."

After they finished the scrumptious meal, Sarah and Lucy helped Abigail clear the dishes from the table.

"The roast beef was just delicious, Abigail."

"Thank you, Lucy. I cooked it slowly, so it would be tender. We were glad the green beans were ready this morning. Mr. Thompson picked them after he dug the new potatoes."

"Perfect timing for our supper this evening." Sarah held the plates in front of her. "I hope Solomon is feeling well. He didn't eat as much as usual."

Abigail nodded. "You're right. He's normally not bashful about second helpings."

Lucy gathered the glasses from the table. "He's not at all what

I expected. You made him sound like a man who grunted instead of talked. You know, like someone who never came out of the woods. Instead, he's jovial and really nice looking."

Sarah breezed past her with an armload of dishes she had collected from the table. "That's good to know, because he thinks you're beautiful."

"He does?"

"Of course, he never sees very many women in the Big Thicket."

Lucy chased Sarah to the kitchen. "Very funny."

Abigail tied her apron around her waist. "I'll put these dishes in some water to soak, and we'll go in the library to visit with everyone."

"Yes, I think I'll let the children stay up a little while since they are enjoying their company tonight. They always enjoy the men in our family, but they seem really eager to be around Andrew. I never expected that."

Abigail nodded. "He has a way with children. I noticed that tonight."

Sarah shrugged. "Imagine that."

Uncle Marshall joined them in the kitchen. "You ladies come on in and visit. We'll get those dishes later."

Laughter erupted from the front of the house. Abigail turned to Sarah and Lucy. "Let's go see what we're missing."

Once they were all seated in the library, Sarah noticed John was very still and rubbed his eyes. She took him in her arms and excused herself from the gathering. He was ready to get bedclothes on.

When she joined the others again a soft glow came from the oil lamps situated on the sconces on the wall. But an even softer glow was in Thomas's eyes while he held Melissa and recounted the story of him and Solomon finding James Watts, wounded and alone in the woods.

"Where did he go when you came here, Solomon?" Hopefully, he was somewhere far away.

Solomon glanced at Thomas. "He's staying for a while with the Cains. Mrs. Cain wants to teach him to read. And Clark Cain says he'll teach him to get by, living off the land."

"I hope he cooperates with them." Thomas smoothed Melissa's long, blonde hair.

"I believe he will. He loves the attention."

Andrew stood and glanced around the room. "I can't tell you how much I enjoyed this tonight." He stared at Sarah. "Thank you, Sarah, for inviting me, but I'd better get on home."

Sarah walked with Andrew to the door. "I want to tell you again how much I appreciate you taking care of Melissa today."

"I'm just thankful I was close by. I'm grateful you let me be with you and the children tonight. Goodnight."

He strode out the door.

Sarah watched him walk away. She felt gratitude and nothing more. But that was a start. Gratitude was better than nothing. Because up until now, besides anger, she felt nothing for him.

Chapter Thirty-Two

Since Thomas was back at the sawmill, Sarah enjoyed the freedom to stay home most days. Even though she spent time working on the upcoming wedding, she mostly enjoyed being with the children, walking to the creek with them or reading a story when they asked. Her greatest joy came from being a mother to Melissa and John, and soon, that measure of joy would only grow, when she could also be a wife to Thomas.

Once the children were in their beds for a nap, Sarah and Abigail sat down at the table in the dining room to make decisions concerning the food to be served at the wedding. Eliza had nearly finished all her work for the day and was sweeping the kitchen floor before she left for home. They didn't want to hamper her efforts in the kitchen, so the conversation included them calling out to her while she worked.

"Eliza, what do you think about fried chicken and corn on the cob? We don't want to just serve cake and punch." Abigail tilted her head and turned her ear toward the kitchen.

"That sounds delicious, but somebody's goin' to be fryin' chicken all the day long if you have as many guests as I think you will."

"That could be a problem, I suppose." Sarah fanned herself with a piece of paper that had laid on the table. "Since it's summer, I think we'll have watermelon, too. How does that sound?"

Abigail chuckled. "Perhaps we should talk more about the food later. I think you're hungry. Let's talk about the dresses for the wedding party for a minute."

"I have the fabric for the dresses for Lucy, Eliza, and Melissa. Once Mrs. Corine finishes my dress, she'll begin on the others. I know the wedding is just three weeks away, but Eliza says Corine has enlisted the help of her niece, who is also a good seamstress, to help with all the dresses besides mine."

Abigail sighed. "I'm so glad I have my dress already. I truly enjoy sewing, so mine is finished. And Marshall will wear the suit he wore in our wedding."

"Everything is going just as planned. Thomas and I will be meeting with Brother Maxwell this week to discuss the ceremony. Since it's not my first marriage, I thought at first we should have a small wedding, maybe family only. But the more I considered it, I realized I feel like everyone here in Pineville is my family."

Charles Griffin appeared in the doorway. "Hello, ladies."

"Hello, Charles. It's rare that you get to come by this time of day. I think I'll go up and check on the children and let you and your mother visit."

"Actually, Sarah, I came to see you. But I'd like for my mother to stay in here."

"Surely. Come on in and take a seat."

Charles entered the room, a stiffness in his movements.

"I think I'd rather stand, if you don't mind." He shifted from one foot to the other one.

"The shipment arrived from Ricco Brothers Funeral Home this morning on the train."

Sarah dropped the pen she was holding, and Abigail steadied the ink bottle before it fell over. Sarah's eyes filled with tears. All the air left her lungs for a moment. "This morning? I had no prior notice. No letter."

Abigail looked to Charles, then back to Sarah. "I don't understand. Shipment?"

Charles chewed on his bottom lip for a bit. "We'll hold it at the depot for now." He stood beside Sarah. "Would you like for me to get Thomas and Marshall to come over?"

Sarah stared straight ahead. "No. I don't want them to have to leave the mill."

She took the list she had been working on and turned it over, face down on the table. "I didn't know how long it would be before I received my husband's remains. Or if I ever would since he had been buried as a pauper."

Abigail embraced Sarah. "Oh, my dear, we had no idea you had contracted to have this done."

"I didn't tell anyone. I presumed I would have notice before they shipped Nils's body. After I received the letter from the police officer in New York notifying me of his death, I contacted the officer and told him I would very much like for Nils's body to be returned home and he referred me to Ricco Brothers Funeral Home. They advised me it would take a while because Hart Island, where Potters Field is located, was not easily accessible. And sometimes, more than one body was placed in a grave."

Sarah wiped her eyes. "Charles, if you can hold Nils's body for now, we will take him to the cemetery first thing in the morning."

Charles turned to leave. "I'll help in any way I can."

"Thank you. Since I've had a moment to gather my thoughts, I realize I do need help from Uncle Marshall and Thomas. We'll need some men to dig the grave, and I think I'd like to have a log wagon for the body and a couple of mules to pull it to the cemetery."

Abigail put her hand to her chest. "Dear, would you like for Brother Maxwell to accompany us to the cemetery, and maybe say a few words?"

"Yes, I think that's a good idea. I always thought I'd receive notice and make arrangements before the remains arrived."

Charles turned his hat around in his hands. "I'm headed to the mill to see Marshall. It's not that long until quitting time now. I'll make sure he comes on home and brings Thomas with him."

"Thank you, Charles."

Sarah picked up the wedding list from the table. "I'll put this away for now." She folded the piece of paper and placed it in her pocket.

"Abigail, I'll be down by the creek bank for a few minutes. I— I need a little time."

Abigail patted Sarah's arm. "Don't you worry. I'll listen for the children and we'll have some teacakes and milk when they wake from their nap."

Sarah nodded and let herself out the back door. She trudged down the beaten path to the creek and sat on a log that jutted out into the water. Now that his physical body was back here at home where it belonged, the reality of his death stung once again. She tilted her head and glanced up at the sky. When she gazed at the sun, it was like his face beamed at her.

She wanted so badly to have him buried in the cemetery in Pineville near her mother and grandparents. This was something she pursued. And now, what she had longed for had come to fruition.

She had not stopped loving Nils, but she had accepted the fact that he would never be with them again in this life. Now, at this moment the wedding plans and the hope of a new life with Thomas were unimportant. Her heart was divided again. When would she ever be able to love with her heart fully mended?

After a long while, Thomas joined her and drew her close. She turned to see Thomas peering at her. "What can I do to help?"

She studied her hands in her lap. "You don't have to be involved in this, you know."

"Yes, I believe I do. I won't let you do this without me by your side." Thomas lowered himself down to the log where she sat. "Marshall is gathering the men to dig the grave now. He needs to know when you want to go to the cemetery with Nils's body."

"I'd like to go shortly after sun up tomorrow morning. We had a nice memorial service when Nils died, so I'd like to quietly take his remains to the final resting place. That way we can move through town before things get too busy and after the mill is already running."

"Let's go on back up to the house. The sun will be setting soon."

Sarah never looked up. "You go on. I'll be there shortly. I need time, Thomas. More time."

Thomas lowered his voice. "Time now? Time before the wedding? What do you mean, Sarah?"

Sarah lifted her head and took in a deep breath. "Time now. Time before we are married." She shook her head. "I'm sorry, Thomas."

He walked back toward the house.

When the shadows grew longer, Sarah stood and straightened her skirt. Her late husband's body had been returned to his family. His children were too young to even realize what had happened. And his wife was up to her neck in wedding plans.

She shivered, even though the air before dusk hung hot and heavy around her.

Sarah walked down the stairs clad in a dark gray broadcloth dress complete with a matching bonnet. She had stopped wearing the dark clothes of a widow but had ended her mourning period prematurely.

The bonnet would protect her from the sun at the cemetery, but it would also hide her face as they made their journey this morning. She knew she had done nothing morally wrong, but she had followed the rules of respect much too loosely. And she had not been brought up that way.

Uncle Marshall had the wagon waiting at the front gate, and she and Abigail made their way to meet him. Eliza came to the door and waved, signaling she had all things covered at home.

Uncle Marshall turned to her. "Like I said earlier, the grave is ready. Charles will drive the wagon carrying Nils's body out to the cemetery, so we'll join him at the depot. Thomas will meet us there and follow on horseback."

Sarah smiled, but the corners of her mouth struggled with the show of expression. She let her uncle help her up in the wagon.

Once the small procession arrived at their destination, they were met by Brother Maxwell with Bible in hand, and Andrew and Dr. Bailey.

When Sarah stepped from the wagon Andrew reached for her hand. Once everyone was situated, he took his place behind her. Uncle Marshall stood on one side of her and Thomas, the other.

She stared at the sturdy pine coffin in front of her. This had been the desire of her heart, to bring her husband home to her and the children so he could rest peacefully there. She had prayed for peace since she discovered Nils was gone. Would she ever feel that comfort?

As soon as the final prayer was said and the coffin was lowered, Thomas moved from Sarah's side and made his way outside the gate to his horse. Blaze didn't move when Thomas took the reins to lead him. Thomas coaxed him a bit so he could lead him away from there. Once he was far enough down the road that the noise wouldn't disrupt the gathering at the cemetery, he would ride to the mill. After all, that was his most important function now.

After the work day ended, he had to break the news to Solomon. No wedding now. Would there ever be one?

Thomas had not talked to Solomon the night before, but he

needed to level with his friend. After all, Solomon needed to get home and plant his sweet potatoes and corn. His existence depended on the efforts he put forth during this season.

And Thomas had to send word to his brother in Amarillo. Paul had surely been happy to hear the wedding would be in June since he and Martha were expecting their first little one come the end of August. The doctor had said she could come by train in June but no later than that.

Thomas hadn't told Sarah about the baby. Paul and Martha planned to come a few days before the wedding, so they could share the news then. He wouldn't tell Sarah now either, because he didn't want to force her into an earlier date. Or a date at all.

Hopefully there would be a wedding in the plans for him and Sarah somewhere down the road. But after today, he didn't have any idea when it would be. Thomas counted himself to be a patient man, but he had stood by and watched Sarah grieve too many times for a man that had left home of his own free will. She said she needed more time. And he would give her that. But was that all she needed?

Chapter Thirty-Three

Sarah made sure the children were asleep, so it was a good time for her to contemplate the events of the last few days. She made her way to the parlor and to her favorite piece of furniture in the room, the settee upholstered in blue brocade fabric. Abigail came into the room, holding Melissa's skirt she was mending.

"Do you mind if I sit with you?"

"No, I'd love your company. I surely appreciate you working on Melissa's skirt. She caught it on the fence, playing hide and seek with John."

"I love to mend. I like to use the smallest stitches I can possibly use, to try to make it look like new. Of course, if you look closely, you can see the rips or tears were there. But, once I mend it, it's useful again and is truly stronger than before."

"Abigail, do you believe our hearts are the same way? Or do you think they ever really mend? Do you think I can love Thomas completely, or will I always have a portion of my heart reserved for Nils?"

Abigail held up the little floral skirt. "I believe our hearts are like this fabric. These stitches show there was a tear that had to be repaired where there was once a completely whole garment. It will be strong once more, but the stitches will always remain. They are a testament to something that happened, something that made the fabric weaker, until it was mended and became complete again. Each time you start to put the skirt on Melissa, you'll see the small stitches and remember." Abigail sighed. "As far as your heart, the

171

stitches will always be there, and you'll have those memories. But your heart will be whole again and ready to love."

Before Sarah could respond, Gus barked and growled on the porch. She made her way to the door and pulled the curtain open at the sidelight. Abigail appeared in the entryway. "Do we have a visitor?"

"Looks like Andrew. He's in his new doctor's carriage. Gus doesn't know him yet, I'm afraid."

Sarah strolled on the porch to greet him. "Good morning. Are you headed this way on a house call?"

Andrew let himself in the gate. "I'm headed on a house call to see you. That is, if you can spare a few minutes."

"I suppose I can. Would you like to visit on the porch?"

Sarah took a seat in the swing while Andrew claimed the nearest chair.

"I don't want to meddle in your affairs, Sarah. And I know you don't want me to. But I care for you more than you can ever imagine."

Sarah looked away then turned back to answer him. "What is it, Andrew?"

His sea green eyes settled on hers. "Have you talked to Thomas since yesterday?"

"No, I haven't yet. I thought I may see him this evening." Sarah peered down at her shoes.

"Please go talk to him. I watched his face yesterday at the cemetery. Since I stood directly behind you, I could see him. He needs you to remind him how much you care for him."

"Why are you so worried about this?" Sarah narrowed her eyes.

"Because I care what your life will be like in the days to come. Thomas is such a good man. He's patient and kind. And he loves my daughter and grandchildren."

"I told him I had to have more time. He understands, I'm sure."

Andrew leaned closer. "Please don't make the mistakes I've made."

Sarah stood to signal the end of the conversation. "How could you suggest such a thing? My children are my life."

"Please sit down and let me finish."

Sarah slowly lowered herself down to the swing.

"As sad as it may be, Nils is gone. But now you have a chance to give your children a happy home, much like they would've had if their father were still here."

Sarah searched Andrew's face to see if she could read a chapter of regrets there.

"Did you have a chance at love again, Andrew? After my mother died?"

He covered his face. "No, I never allowed such a thought. I held myself responsible for her death, even after I'd done everything I knew to do." He shook his head. "Besides, I've never met a woman who can hold a candle to Katherine. Never."

Andrew looked at Sarah and smiled. "I've seen you with Thomas, and I know you love him. I'm asking that you try to make a decision about how much time you need and then tell him today."

Sarah sighed. "Looks like I've been very selfish, haven't I? I didn't mean it that way at all. It's just been so hard, reconciling my feelings with the man I married first and the man I'll soon marry."

She stood and hugged him. "Thank you for helping me with this. I always felt I should wait a year before I married after Nils died, and then I shifted away from my heartfelt plans. Thomas never pressured me, it was all of my own doing."

Andrew's eyes glistened. "I'd be happy to escort you over to the sawmill in my new carriage. You'll love the leather seat."

"And I'd be happy to have you escort me. Give me a minute to tell Abigail and Eliza."

Sarah made her way to the front door. Her step was lighter after heeding advice from her father.

Once she spoke with Abigail, she checked her hair in the mirror in the entryway and met Andrew on the porch. "Thank you for reminding me to take Thomas's feelings into consideration. I've been neglectful in that area."

"You've had a lot of things to work through. My appearing in town hasn't made your life easier, for sure. And besides, I really want to help. I know you don't want to hear this, but I love you very much."

Sarah nodded. "I'm not ready for those sentiments yet, but I'm hopeful that I will be someday."

Before he reached the gate, Andrew stopped in his tracks. "Oh, I have something for you. Your grandmother's basket. That day we met in the cemetery, you dropped it when you left. Then I brought it to you when we talked at Benjamin's office. And you left it again."

"Who told you it was my grandmother's?"

"No one told me. Your mother and I gave it to her. There was a lady in San Jacinto County who made the nicest pine baskets. We had that made especially to hold flowers." Andrew smiled. "When we knew we were expecting a baby, we came to Pineville to visit. Katherine and I brought your grandmother roses in that basket. You know, to celebrate the good news. It was Katherine's idea, of course. She always was so thoughtful."

"Oh, my. I never knew. I wonder why my grandmother never told me? Perhaps it had a meaning to her that she thought I'd never comprehend."

"Your grandmother probably tried to shield you from much of her grief, just as you've done with the children after you lost Nils. I have a feeling that the basket was something she loved, since it came from her sweet daughter. But it had to be bittersweet, too."

"You're probably right about that. It began as a symbol of joy, then the flowers she carried in it a few times a year were for her daughter's grave. My grandmother had to miss my mother so much."

The two of them walked in silence to his sleek, new buggy. They started out and his horse moved down the dirt roads almost effortlessly. Before long, they arrived at the sawmill.

"I'll stay out here and wait. Take your time."

She wiped her hands on her dress then started to the door of the office. What if he was not ready to see her? What if he felt like she had alienated him one too many times?

When she entered the building and saw him walking with Clyde toward his office, her heart leaped a little.

He stared at Sarah for a minute. "Clyde, we'll talk later."

He smiled and moved to stand beside her. "Sarah, what brings you here this morning?"

"You. Could we talk for a few minutes?"

"Of course. Let's go in my office."

When they reached his office, Sarah motioned to the chair in front of the desk. "May I sit down?"

"Sure. I'm just kind of confused, though." He sat on the edge of the desk nearest her chair. "The other day you said you needed time. Then yesterday at the cemetery, you pretty much ignored the fact that I was there." Thomas rubbed his forehead. "I know you are sad. I understand that. But when I try to help, you push me away."

"I know. That's why I'm here. I'd like to ask your forgiveness. I feel awful."

Thomas touched her hand. "I didn't mean to rush you about the wedding. I was impatient. When I was gone those two months, I missed you so much."

"And I missed you." She bowed her head. "I wanted to wait until Nils had been gone a year, out of respect for his memory and for the fact that he is Melissa and John's father. Then I was the one who decided a June wedding would be lovely. Remember?"

Thomas sighed. "I say we wait until September. It will be a

little over a year then since Nils died. And I think you will be more comfortable with that. Or if you need more time, please tell me."

Her eyes brightened. "No, that's perfect. Come September, we'll finally be husband and wife."

She looked at the man she loved. Her heart beat like it was hammering away, covering crevices deep within. The stitches were there, but this heart of hers was mending, once and for all.

Epilogue

Three Months Later
September 1907

Sarah pulled the curtain back ever so slightly and peered at the scene below. "Abigail, you have the best ideas. The benches are perfect in the yard. And the matching arbor is beautiful."

"Well, this is a very special wedding. You and Thomas are creating a new life all your own. And a wedding ceremony that's your own is a good way to begin. I'm glad you decided against having it at the church, since your other ceremony was there."

Sarah let the curtain fall back in place. "Yes, I'm glad we decided to have it here at home. And we couldn't have asked for more beautiful weather than we've had on this day. I see that Brother Maxwell is already down there, making sure everything is ready. And Mr. Martin appears to be tuning his fiddle, even though I can't hear a sound."

The door opened and Lucy stepped inside, followed by Eliza. "Everything is in perfect order downstairs. I say it's time to get dressed."

Eliza squeezed Sarah's hand. "Hattie Ruth did a wonderful job on the food. She's not going to want to see another piece of a chicken for the rest of her life, though. The corn on the cob is boiling and she said the yeast rolls will cook during the ceremony, so they'll be hot and ready for the butter."

Abigail nodded. "And our friend, Nellie, outdid herself on the wedding cake. It is absolutely beautiful."

Lucy gazed dreamily into the distance. "I want her to make my cake when I get married."

"We have to find you a prospective husband first." Sarah winked at her friend.

Abigail stepped to the middle of the group. "I'm going down to fetch Melissa and John so we can dress them. We've put that chore off as long as we can."

Eliza shook her head. "Ruthie and Tillie aren't gonna want them to leave. Would you tell Frank to take them on outside?"

"Sure. Melissa is probably curious about what we're doing up here, but John will want to stay and play with your children, Eliza." Abigail laughed.

Sarah touched Eliza's arm. "Why don't you let the girls come on up? We can send them down to Frank just before the ceremony begins."

"Why thank you, Sarah. They would enjoy being a part of everything. As long as they don't try to distract Melissa too much." Eliza chuckled. "You know how our children can be when they get together."

Sarah shook her head. "And I'm sure we were much the same."

Eliza made her way downstairs and Abigail turned to face Sarah. "The flowers are so lovely. That was such a thoughtful thing that Andrew did, having them shipped from Houston."

"Yes, I appreciate it so much. Once we changed the wedding from June to September, our choices of fresh flowers blooming in the piney woods was slim. I didn't want to use black-eyed susans." Sarah sat on the bed for a moment. "I do appreciate him, Abigail. I'm thrilled that he enjoys the children so much and that they are getting to know him. Your idea of him walking in with the flower girl and ring bearer was a great one. That way he feels like he's a part of our special day and he can also keep John in line."

Lucy moved to sit beside Sarah. "Everything you're doing

today is so lovely. And you are the most beautiful bride, Sarah. You are beaming."

Eliza burst through the door with her twin daughters and Melissa. "John didn't want to come. Your Uncle Marshall said to send John's clothes downstairs, and he'll get him dressed. Said he didn't need to be up here with all these women anyway."

Abigail shook her head. "He's right. I'll take his clothes downstairs."

Eliza cleared her throat. "Oh, and Mr. Smith wants to see you downstairs in the front parlor for a minute, Sarah. He said it's very important."

"Oh, my. Well, I guess I can spare just a minute before I get dressed. But where is Thomas? He can't see me before the wedding."

Eliza's eyes widened. "No ma'am."

Abigail stood by the door to the bedroom with John's clothes. "I'll make sure Thomas is out of the way before you go down. I'll let you know when it's safe."

Sarah glanced around the room. "All I really have to do is put on my wedding dress. I had a luxurious bath this morning with the most soothing lavender soap. Then Beulah Maxwell came over and worked on my hair until it was just the way we thought it should be." Sarah turned around, so they could see the spiral curls in her long brown hair. "The small hat with the veil will fit perfectly."

Abigail marched into the room. "You can come down to the parlor. I have Thomas locked away in the library."

Sarah moved down the stairs just like she usually did if the children weren't with her, taking two steps at a time. She was keenly aware that the next trip down these stairs would be to stand before the man she loved and be joined in matrimony.

When she reached the entryway, she caught sight of Andrew pacing in front of the parlor door.

"Did you need to see me?"

He turned and smiled. "Yes. It will only take a moment of your time. Come in here, please."

Sarah followed him into the front parlor, and he closed the door behind her. "I have something I've saved for you." His eyes filled with tears, and his bottom lip quivered. "I'm so happy you allowed me to be a part of your wedding day." He opened a small velvet box and turned it to Sarah, so she could see the contents. "I bought this for your mother to wear on our wedding day. I'd like for you to wear it today to honor her memory. I'm so sorry she's not here with us."

Sarah covered her mouth and gasped. "Oh, Andrew, it's beautiful. The diamonds are exquisite. Of course I'll wear it, and I'll treasure it always."

She studied his face for a moment. "Would you please help me put it on?"

His hands shook a little, but he nodded. "Certainly. I'd love to."

Once it was in place, she touched it and loved the feel of the cut diamonds, encased in metal, cool against her chest. "I will wear it with such joy."

She turned to leave the room, then stopped. "The flowers are the most beautiful I've ever seen. They've made this day even more special than I imagined."

"White roses for your bouquet signify a new beginning. And the red ones were your mother's favorite, so there's an ample supply of those."

She leaned over and kissed him on the cheek. "I'm so happy to have you here and to be able to share the memories of my mother. This is indeed a wonderful day."

With her heart full she went upstairs where Melissa waited in her beautiful pink lace dress. "Oh, honey, you're just the prettiest flower girl I've ever seen."

Melissa grinned and ran to her mother and hugged her.

Abigail approached Sarah with the wedding dress on a hanger. "Time to put it on, so we can make sure everything is where it should be."

"Before I finish dressing, I must show y'all what Andrew presented me with just now." Sarah patted the diamond necklace. "This belonged to my mother. He gave it to her to wear on their wedding day."

Abigail wiped away a tear, and Lucy and Eliza moved closer to take a look.

"It is a fine piece of jewelry. But just to think it belonged to your mother, why that's so wonderful." Lucy hugged Sarah.

Sarah returned to the window and peeked at the scene below. "Look, Beulah took some of the red roses and worked them into the greenery on the arbor. And the potted ferns at the bottom finish it off perfectly."

She closed the curtain. "I'm ready to get dressed. The hour has finally arrived, hasn't it? There were times I wondered if this day would ever come."

She brushed her hand across the pale blue duchess satin on the dress and the point lace that adorned the bodice and the sleeves just past the elbow. "I couldn't have had a more beautiful dress, even if I'd had it specially made in New Orleans."

Eliza touched the sleeve. "Auntie Corine put her heart into it."

"As she did with all the dresses." Sarah gazed at the pink crepe de chine with a chiffon overlay that Lucy had on and the same dress in a pale yellow that Eliza wore. "You ladies look stunning. When I asked Mrs. Corine for elegant simplicity, she did a wonderful job."

Abigail removed Sarah's dress from the hanger and helped her pull it over her head. "Now, relax while I button these twenty-five satin covered buttons down the back."

Sarah closed her eyes for a moment and stroked the diamond necklace that laid perfectly above the neckline of her dress.

Dipping down in the V-neck of the dress, it was as though the dress was designed to be worn with this particular necklace, or that the necklace had been purchased for this very dress.

Once the buttons were all finished, Sarah turned to face everyone in the room. "Well, if you'll help me with my headpiece and veil, we'll start down the stairs."

Abigail pinned the small satin hat to Sarah's hair and pulled the short veil over her face.

A knock sounded on the door. Eliza called out, "Who is it?"

"It's me, Marshall. I need to see Sari out here."

She met him in the hall. "You're the most beautiful bride I've seen since Abigail." He winked and pointed into the room behind them.

"Why thank you, Uncle Marshall. You are looking mighty handsome yourself."

He took his handkerchief from his pocket and wiped his forehead. "I need to discuss something with you. I think you should ask Andrew to escort you in today. He's just so proud to be here that I feel bad about him not being in the place of honor."

Sarah tapped her foot a few times. "I understand how you feel, but I'm not going to get married today if you don't escort me." Sarah smiled. "I'll tell you what we can do. You walk on my right side, and I'll let him walk on my left side. I'll have two escorts, but you must be one of them."

A huge grin spread across her uncle's face. "I just can see he's aching to do it. And I'll let him give you away."

"Remember, I said I didn't want to be given away this time. This is my second marriage and it's not necessary. I already told Brother Maxwell to leave that part out."

"Well, I think you need to let him do it. You're his only daughter. Take my word for it, you'll be glad you did it this way."

Sarah hugged him. "You are the kindest man. If you can let Brother Maxwell know I've changed my mind, then he can include the giving away part."

She let herself back in the room with the others. "Well, I guess it's time for you all to go downstairs. I'll wait here for my signal to come down."

Lucy stood at the window now, looking below. "Eliza, the gift tables are already nearly full. You get to stand beside all those beautiful things and touch them before anyone else."

"I'm truly honored to have this opportunity to be a part of your wedding." Eliza and Sarah met in an embrace.

Lucy wasn't finished with her commentary on things below. "This Solomon Brown is a handsome man. And I get to walk with him. He's so different from what I imagined."

"And you'll have plenty of time to talk with him after the wedding, Lucy. He's staying on a little while to take care of things at Thomas's place while we spend a few days in New Orleans."

Sarah peered at the wedding preparations once more. "He came. I'm so happy for Thomas." She turned to face the others with tears forming in her eyes.

Lucy jerked the curtain back again. "Who? Oh, it's Paul. Thank goodness. I know Thomas will be so glad his brother is here.

Abigail clapped her hands. "Ladies, it's time to go downstairs. All the guests are waiting, so we'd better get started."

Eliza gathered Ruthie and Tillie on either side of her. "We're going down. When I talk to you again, you'll be Mrs. Sarah Carson. I'm so happy for you."

Sarah hugged Eliza. "Thank you...for everything."

Sarah leaned down and kissed her little daughter before she walked away with Abigail. What a wonderful day. All of her family and friends were here with her, and she would soon be married to Thomas, the man she loved so dearly.

She stood by the door, enjoying the sounds of the preparation going on down below her. Abigail's voice rose above the others. "Lucy, you will walk out first, then Melissa and John. And

Andrew, there's been a change. You aren't walking with the children. You'll be helping Marshall walk Sarah down the aisle. Yes, I'm sure, Andrew. I'm sure."

The front door opened, and Lucy walked on the porch and toward Solomon who stood outside to escort her. Abigail was the only voice she heard below now. "Melissa, John, I'll walk part of the way with you, then you'll just walk like we practiced. And follow Miss Lucy, she'll help you."

Sarah knew this was her cue. She started carefully down the stairs, holding her skirt a little above her ankles.

She did not plan to shed a tear, but the two men waiting for her dabbed at the corners of their eyes with handkerchiefs. Mr. Martin played "Here Comes the Bride" on the fiddle, and she motioned to her escorts to begin.

Sarah walked slowly, savoring this wedding march. She caught sight of Thomas standing between Brother Maxwell and Solomon. His dark eyes met hers, but through their darkness, light danced and shone through the surface, and matched the motion of his smile.

Once the three of them reached the front, Brother Maxwell addressed them. "Who gives this woman to be married to this man?" Andrew looked upward for a few seconds before he proclaimed, "Her mother and I do."

Sarah lifted her veil and kissed Andrew's cheek, and she felt her mother's presence for a lingering moment. Her vision of her with her parents was whole again. Andrew took his place on the bench beside Abigail.

She turned and hugged her Uncle Marshall and kissed his cheek, too, knowing he deserved all the love a true father could ever hope for. He turned and sat on the bench beside Abigail, closest to the aisle.

Such a peace washed over her when she joined Thomas in front of Brother Maxwell and the rest of the wedding party. To her surprise, the children joined them. This arrangement had not been planned but it was symbolic of their love and their family now, so she and Thomas pulled each of them in closer.

Finally, she was asked the question she had waited for. "Sarah Andersson, do you take Thomas Carson to be your husband?"

She studied his face. "Yes, I do. With all my heart."

Brother Maxwell proclaimed, "I now pronounce you man and wife. What therefore God hath joined together, let not man put asunder."

Thomas and Sarah shared a kiss amid near deafening applause, coupled with a few ear-piercing whistles from the mill hands. John covered both ears before Thomas scooped him up in his arms. Sarah took Melissa's hand and the four of them made their way down the aisle formed between the row of benches.

Just for a moment, Sarah thought her heart may burst wide open when she moved forward with Thomas and her precious children. The four of them glided through the crowd that gathered around them, eager to begin their journey, their life together, as a family.

Acknowledgments

Much appreciation to—

My family, for always supporting and encouraging me.

My editor, Liz Tolsma, for sharing your expertise and for bearing with the vernacular and abundant use of double prepositions from this East Texan.

Crystal Barnes, for the beautiful cover, fantastic formatting and patience throughout the process.

My readers, for joyfully joining me on this journey. You'll never know how much your comments and kind words spurred me on to complete this story.

Marilyn

About the Author

MARILYN PEVETO is a lifelong East Texan from a family that has lived in the Piney Woods for generations. Growing up hearing tales of sawmills at the turn of the twentieth century made the region's history a natural setting for her stories.

Her hobbies include reading, browsing in antique stores for her next treasure, and cooking her family's favorite Southern foods.

Marilyn enjoys life with her two adult children, a son-in-law, an adorable granddaughter, her husband of forty-two years, and her faithful writing partners, a little white dog and a geriatric beagle.

51269339R00112

Made in the USA
Columbia, SC
17 February 2019